D0021595

The Rap Factor

By the same author:

Nana
Diva
Luna
Lola
Vida
Alba

THE ATLANTIC MONTHLY PRESS
NEW YORK

Delacorta
Translated by Catherine Texier

THE RAP
FACTOR

Copyright © 1993 by Delacorta

Translated by Catherine Texier

Published simultaneously in Canada

Printed in the United States of America

Library of Congress Cataloging-in-Publication Data

Delacorta, 1945–

The rap factor: novel / Delacorta; translated by Catherine

Texier.

ISBN 0-87113-529-9

I. Title.

PQ2675.D5R36 1993   843'.914—dc20   92-35562

DESIGN BY LAURA HOUGH

The Atlantic Monthly Press

19 Union Square West

New York, NY 10003

FIRST PRINTING

to rap queens and kings

1

I was at the Palace, sitting on the terrace. It was three P.M., a gentle breeze was blowing in from the ocean, and the temperature was pushing a pleasant eighty-five. Gloria waltzed in with my favorite breakfast: a bowl of yogurt with mango, cantaloupe, papaya, strawberries, almonds, and raisins, and a banana muffin, fresh and unctuous like her, like her dark eyes, like the juicy tenderness of her body that she paraded before me.

I was waiting for the strong and pungent coffee to hit my veins.

"Hi, Zulu. Aren't you reading your mail this morning?"

"I am in a meditative mood."

"Suzy told me that you deserve your reputation."

"Yes, ma'am, I am the best detective in the state of Florida . . ."

"She said you were the best lay on the Gulf of Mexico."

"Leave me your phone number, but let me tell you up front, I am rarely free until five A.M."

"Anytime."

"Isn't Gloria the name of a hurricane . . ."

She flashed a smile that could have struck an alligator dead, and petted my hair. The palm trees came into focus. I love women of action. My body pulsed with energy. Gloria let out a laugh that came from deep inside her womb and waltzed on to take the order of a skinny photographer whose Armani glasses almost made him look brainy.

My cellular phone whistled.

"Hi, it's Brad. There's a Club meeting tonight. Three A.M."

"Okeydokey, copper. Who's in charge of the nourishment?"

"Joe, he just called me."

"Later."

Gloria wrote her phone number on a paper napkin. She slipped a strawberry between my lips. Then another. And another. Petra, a Polish homeless woman who walked by every day, stopped at my table. I gave her ten dollars and kissed her hand. She offered me a cigar, a Macanudo. I put it aside for later.

"Working on a new case, pretty boy?"

"It's too early yet. I'm waiting."

She sized up the other customers with a professional eye and muttered:

"All these cheapskates. Waste of time."

She walked away singing a Marvin Gaye hit, "Sexual Healing." She was a classy dame. A few dark clouds drifted by to remind the locals they were not in California, but in Miami, the most beautiful and hottest city in the world. Below me, on the sand, a shy model surrounded by an entourage of assistants, makeup artists, and hangers-on was waiting for the master, a fat and sunburnt bozo in Bermuda shorts. He had himself sprayed with antiburn lotion before condescending to stare into his viewfinder. A fine, dark blue line joined the turquoise ocean to the sky. A hot number on roller skates glided by, showing off a proud ass. The creature, whose cutoff jeans had been ripped by an exhibitionist's hand, braked in front of me, drained my glass of water, winked, and swung her happy muscles back into action.

Gloria refilled my coffee cup.

"Little does she know that blonds don't stand a chance with you . . ."

"They taste of the supermarket. I'd rather eat ghetto pussy."

Gloria: *"We want some pussy!"*

Me: *"We want some pussy!"*

After this little early-morning rap in honor of 2 Live Crew, I was ready to answer the second call of the day.

"Mr. Ignazio Talawapi Alonzo Marwin Utusha Tenero?"

"Himself, live, at your service, but please call me Zulu for short."

"Delighted. You were recommended to me at the Multiple Sclerosis garden party given by the mayor. What, may I ask, is your rate?"

"Two thousand a day, plus expenses, for a basic job. Double that when I have to risk my life. The client pays for lost bullets, so to speak."

"That's outrageous!"

"I am the most expensive PI in the city of Miami, ma'am. Three days paid up front, nonreturnable."

"You must have a fabulous office, a private plane, a dream house, a boat, gorgeous secretaries . . ."

"Nope. No roadster, no hat, no trench coat, no dirty

office with the sun filtering through the venetian blinds, not even a bottle of bourbon."

"Glad to hear you don't drink."

"Tell me what this is about."

"It's a delicate matter."

"Your husband?"

"Well . . . yes . . . he entertains . . ."

"Sinful relationships?"

"So to speak."

"Anybody will do the job for a hundred a day. I don't deal with sex. I believe in sexual freedom."

"I am prepared to pay."

"Are you aware of the fact that I am not white?"

"Ah . . . No one told me . . ."

"I am a cultural megamix."

"A what?"

"My grandmother is black, my grandfather Seminole Indian, and my father married the daughter of a Cuban and a white woman."

"Interesting . . ."

"No kidding."

"Do you have a detective license?"

"I studied at Yale. I have a Ph.D. in criminology and a B.A. in comparative literature. Is that good enough for you?"

"How old are you?"

"In my thirties, ma'am. Have you by any chance read Thoreau's *Walden*?"

"*Wal* . . ."

"It's the story of a guy who's had it with society and retires to a cabin by a pond. There he learns—"

"You know I could have your license revoked. I have friends in the district attorney's office."

"Why don't you go out and buy a copy of *Nasty As They Wanna Be* and hire yourself a gigolo. I can provide you with a list of phone numbers if you'd like."

I hung up. My cup of coffee was being refilled for the third time and Gloria's breasts stood an inch away from my face. I rubbed my forehead against them.

"Hip!"

"Hop!"

"It's our culture!"

Lita pulled up at the wheel of my tan BMW convertible with leather interior. A cool girl, Lita. She never opened the door, but with the grace of a feline lifted herself out of the car under the stares of the bemused passersby. Lita was twenty-seven, a pure ghetto flower. Next to her was Roy, the other half of my team, fifteen years old, a B-boy I had caught trying to steal my wheels some six months earlier. I had given him a licking. French boxing (I am an adept) against his kung fu—he didn't stand a chance. I immediately hired him. Since then he slept in the Beemer and made seventy-five dollars a day. He was my eyes when I indulged myself with a mini nap, my private deejay, my African shadow. This homeboy knew every corner of the city inside out.

Lita, on the other hand, had gotten the job for a number of reasons: she could diddle with my car computer, which was hooked to the police mainframe, like an expert; she was shrewd, sharp, smart, snappy, a stunner; she had full knowledge of every compact disk in my trunk, danced like an Apsaras (she could swing her ass to any kind of rap, funk, or reggae beat, not to mention kick her sublime gams up in the air), and could hold her own with me (after a few lessons) in French boxing. Her beauty served as a lure to foil enemies. Her grandmother, a *bruja,* cured me when I got sick. And last but not least, Lita carried my blaster so that I could keep both hands free. She made one hundred bucks a day. Roy, Lita, and I were like the Holy Trinity, three in one. We didn't fuck each other, but that notwithstanding, everything between us ran as smoothly as synchronized orgasms.

Every morning they pulled up at the curb as I was sipping my third cup of coffee. They could find me anywhere. Armani gaped as these two creatures came up to me and sat down at my table. Lita sported black bicycle shorts and a red leotard. Roy, a baseball cap screwed backwards, yellow and blue, hip-hop from head to toe. Too colorful for words, both of them.

"Good afternoon, Live Crew . . ."

Boss! Boss!
Yo! You the boss!
Class! Class!
Yo! Boss, you got class!
Word.
What goes around Miami
Comes back to us
'Cause, yo! Boss!
You the Boss! You the Boss!
Crew! Crew! Live, Live Crew!
If you the Boss,
Then I'm the King
Of the sticky fingers
Roy. Word.
You badass partner!
Lita! Lita!
She the Kicker,
Yo! Agile Feet,
Such sweet meat,

Smash the tough guys,
Turn on the B-boys,
Yo! Boss!
You and me and she—we the team!
In the hot moist jungle of Mia-mi!
We the team! We the team!
Live Crew! Live Crew! Live, Live Crew!

"Come on, homey, what you want for breakfast?" whispered Gloria.

Gimme waffles
Eggs and toasts.
Don't delay,
Don't make no boasts.
Jelly orange,
Juicy juice.
That's Zulu's favorite,
Pure black juicy juice.
Luscious orange juice for me
Because I'm free.
Orange juice to give me strength
'Cause I'm the Roy,
I'm the boy.
Roy! Roy!
Boy-toy! Roooooy!
I'm the boy,
Roy! Roy!
Boy-toy! Roy!

"What about you, Lita?"
"A strawberry milk shake and French toast, please."

Lita turned to me.

"What's happening, man?"

"Pretty quiet this morning."

"You should chant, man."

Case! Case! Case! Case!
Where is our casey-case?
Case! Case! Case! Case!
We need a casey-case.
Case! Case! Case! Case!
If we don't get no casey-case . . .
Case! Case! Case! Case!
We in the street . . .
Case! Case! Case! Case!
We need a customer . . .

"Lita, don't ever mention chanting in front of this crazy fuck again!"

"Yo, don't be provoking me, man!"

Gloria brought Roy's eggs. He built up his strength in silence. Lita looked rested; her copper-colored skin had a peaceful glow, contrasting with her burning eyes. She sipped her milk shake and drowned her French toast under a thick coat of maple syrup.

Every morning, for openers, we decided on our music program.

"What do we start with?"

"Ice Cube is cool."

Finally the phone whistled.

"Yo . . ."

"Zulu?"

"Yo . . ."

"It's Princess Bashma . . ."

"You're the best, Bashma!"

"They're trying to do me in . . ."

"Where are you?"

"1215 NW Fifty-seventh."

Roy stuffed the rest of his breakfast between two paper plates. I was already behind the wheel. Lita popped in Princess Bashma's latest CD, *Serious Tits,* the BMW sound system kicked in, a marvel of technology that roared with six hundred watts of power bass notes as we sped down Collins Avenue.

Three minutes later, we were surrounded by islands where the rich anchored their yachts in front of opulent mansions half hidden behind bougainvilleas, wisteria, and jasmine. The lawns were smoother than a carpet. A few magnolia petals lay on the grass, looking like water lilies floating on a pond.

On the pier, Cubans, Chicanos, and blacks were trying to catch dinner and complained about the monster outboards that troubled their waters. In lieu of successful angling, the fishermen could at least get an eyeful of the charming pale sirens displayed on the boats' decks.

Downtown, on our right, the huge Sears building looked like an enormous cream puff. The BMW tires squealed with the acceleration. When we got to the freeway, I pressed down the gas pedal while Princess Bashma's fabulous voice spat a rap as sharp as a piranha's teeth. Roy was gulping down the last of his waffle and rapping along with Bashma's lyrics. Finally, he couldn't take it any longer:

"Fuck, man! Bust a move. Bashma's in trouble! The sister is a fucking goddess!"

I was already going 120, a bit above the speed limit, but since I was already exceeding it, what the hell, I pushed the engine up to 140.

2

Eighteen minutes later we crashed like a meteorite into the heart of Paradise City, the Miami ghetto with the sweet-sounding name. Hell, but not without its charms; the most dangerous neighborhood in the city, bursting with crack houses, drug dealers, guns, gangs, hookers, and pimps. Paradoxically, if you had connections, it was the safest place in the city. You could walk the streets with a bazooka stuck under your arm, and no one would give you as much as a double take. People would just melt from your line of sight, and that would be the end of it.

Stomping on the brakes, I skidded to a stop in front of Princess Bashma's apartment. It was a three-story building, pink, not overly run down, surrounded by burnt vegetation, like all gardens in poor Miami neighborhoods, since water was being rationed. In South Florida, one had to believe in miracles: apparently, rain fell only on rich people's lawns. It was even forbidden to wash your car, and I found myself wondering if Roy used Perrier or Evian on mine.

Roy and Lita checked to make sure the coast was clear while I ran up the stairs. The house was dead silent. Amazing how when there's trouble the neighbors always find an aunt to visit, a card game to finish, or the urgent need to hit the liquor store for a fifth. The door was open. I pushed my gun inside and when nothing moved, I followed.

Princess Bashma was lying naked on the aqua carpet. A two- or three-year-old little girl was sitting next to her, in a green dress, her braids tied with red ribbons, crying. Princess Bashma hadn't been dead long. She was still warm, soft, and perfumed. Only her expression seemed pained. It looked as if she'd been poisoned. I ran my hands over her face trying to fill myself with her mystery, as if one day the memory of that gesture would bring me an answer. I always thought that the dead deserved a little tenderness, so I gave them as much as I could—that is, if they hadn't tried to kill me.

Bashma was one of the most stunning pieces of ebony I had ever laid eyes on. Cone-shaped breasts, a delicate waist, a supple stomach revealing the line of some discreet muscle buildup, a voluptuous and round pubis. She hadn't been raped by the Lord's ways. The little girl stopped crying. Bashma smelled of lilies. Her body lay like a sculpture flooded with light. I carefully examined what I could see of her body. No needle mark, no trace of external violence. I looked inside her mouth. She had a beautiful pink tongue and perfectly aligned teeth. I stroked her face, massaged it to erase the signs of pain, of panic, turning Bashma once again into the gorgeous twenty-three-year-old princess she had been, a ghetto orchid suckled on rap.

Something surprised me. The apartment was completely empty. Even the shelves had been torn off the walls. The little girl was watching me with huge black eyes. I walked around the apartment. The kitchen had also been cleaned out. All that was left were bewildered ants. I could imagine killers snatching the TV, the stereo, the CDs, even some clothes, but this was overly zealous.

Back in the living room, I turned Bashma over. I had seen one side of her; the other side might teach me something. She had a fabulous ass, with a strange peculiarity: a CD was stuck to it: *Felony,* her first album. I took the little girl in my arms, picked up the CD, and went back to Live Crew. I slipped the disk into the CD player. It was my only clue. Roy shed a tear for his fallen idol. He hadn't seen anything outside the building.

Even a dead princess has a family. I consulted with Roy.

"So, Doctor Rap, what do you know about Bashma?"

"According to the latest issue of *Rap Monster,* her favorite hangout was an after-hours bar called the Platinum. The kid must be her daughter, Melody."

"Any boyfriend?"

"A deejay called Acid Profile—he's got a job at Clean Bug. They open early, around ten P.M. He was only the latest; she got laid a lot."

"Amtrak?"

"Maybe. There's a direct reference in the third cut."

Roy fast-forwarded and found the song he'd alluded to: an apologia for group sex, a Miami specialty.

"Shall I call the cops?" Lita asked, already punching our code into the computer.

"Yo, we got to give them some work. Send the message directly to Brad. Ask for all the lab work. She must have been poisoned."

"What are we going to do until tonight?"

"We're going to go see my pal Stuff at Bass Echo. I have an idea."

I called him on his direct line and asked him to wait for me at his office. He was one of these guys who are always on their way to a pussy meeting.

Lita took the wheel, but she couldn't quite control the Beemer at high speed. I tutored her on the way. Even Live Crew needs the benefit of continuing education. Princess Bashma's pure and hard voice on the sound system felt like a scalpel tickling the small of my back. Even at lightning speed, her diction was impeccable. She didn't have to take the backseat to any macho man, no matter how big his mike.

On the highway, near the airport, we got picked up by police radar and a cruiser came after us. We were barely going 130. The cops, two young punks with their hair slicked back, were ready to draw their guns, basic caution at Babylon Beach.

"Papers . . ."

"Hot set of wheels, huh, bro?" Roy said, screwing the bill of his baseball cap forward.

The second cop grabbed him, pulled him out of the car, and opened his legs with his stick. Roy, as flexible as an eel, did a split in front of the astonished cop.

"What the fuck have we got here, a star ballerina?"

We had no time to waste with greenhorns, so I showed them the computer.

"What are you trying to tell me, you're one of us . . . ?"

"Yep, directly connected to the mainframe. So, unless you want to be whipped up by Magimix"—that was Brad's nickname—"you better charm the pants off of us."

One of the cops ran a check on us and came back, sour as a pickle.

" 'Scuse us, Mr. Zulu, we're new in the squad. Great music you're listening to . . ."

"Princess Bashma," Lita said, engulfing them in a cloud of dust.

I was the only PI in Miami who had access to the cops, and you better believe I used it. Of course, information went both ways.

Stuff's office was on Washington Avenue, in a Spanish-style building. Lita and Roy stayed outside with the kid to buy her some doughnuts. As baby-sitters, they were running out of ideas.

There was a new receptionist. Stuff hired a new one every week. This one was a tall redhead with a leather miniskirt and a Frank Zappa T-shirt.

"I see you have a taste for baroque music, hon. Tell Stuff Zulu is on his way," I said, walking through the office.

This redhead smelled like pussy on fire. I mentally put her down on my waiting list. Stuffy's office was a mess, even more than usual, but although he looked like a space cadet, his brain worked fast.

"What's up, Zulu?"

"Princess Bashma. Do you have any pix of her?"

"Only about a couple of pounds."

He swung his ass around on his imperial swivel chair, pulled out a file, and tossed it across his desk. Everything was there, including family snapshots.

"Who's the charming little rosebud?"

"Melody, her daughter."

"And that one?"

"Mona, her sis. She works at the Fruit Market."

"Whereabouts?"

"Dunno exactly."

I finally got to some interesting material, a series of

photos shot in Princess Bashma's apartment. On aqua background, perfect setting for her naked beauty, plus all the furni-
ture and the equipment. It must have taken a hell of a lot of time
for the killers to have moved everything out.

"Can I take these?"

"If you bring them back . . ."

"Here's a scoop for you. Bashma's been done."

"No shit . . ."

"I don't know what happened yet."

"Holy shit, *Rolling Stone* just asked me for a piece on
her."

"Cynical bastard . . ."

"I do what I can."

"Give me the redhead's phone number."

"Foxy little number, huh? . . . The flames of hell . . ."

"What's her name?"

"Galaxy."

"I think I'm about to fire my rocket."

"Love your threads, dude."

"Giorgio. Linen."

"Expensive?"

"Two G's."

On my way back, I stopped by at the flames of hell's
desk.

"Galaxy, how about starting my countdown?"

"Ten . . . nine . . . eight . . . seven . . . You know how
to count to zero?"

"Once you get there time slows down."

"That's the way I like it."

She fired off her most beautiful smile. Going down the
stairs I felt like an astronaut. Outside I reunited with my team.
Melody's lips were full of sugar and she smiled. I swallowed an

orange juice across the street and bought a mango for Melody.

I used a dry cleaner's called Beach Pressing as my personal storage. I dropped by to change into fresh clothes, a puce-colored silk suit with matching pumps, and we turned around back toward Paradise City. I knew the perfect spot to think, the library. I borrowed a couple of novels while I was there. The librarian, a real side of a mountain, had always made me feel welcome. I had saved one of her kids from crack by taking him to the morgue. Roy had got the message too.

With Scotch tape and scissors I reconstructed Bashma's apartment. Roy made a detailed list of its contents.

"This is all going to show up on the floating market, sooner or later," Roy said. He had his connections there.

The floating market was a closed and dangerous fencing operation held each night near a canal. At dawn, all the merchandise vanished, as if by magic.

The list included a few hundred CDs, a top-of-the-line sound system, photos of rappers, a collection of hats, shoes in every color of the rainbow, a synthesizer, a set of drums, African and Brazilian percussions, a plaster hamburger, a gold record, a family photo, an African mask, a Japanese clock, multicolored condoms in a fish tank, a mythology dictionary and several books on the same subject, the inevitable Joseph Campbell tomes, an inflatable alligator that was probably used as a float by Melody, a pizza on a low table, a bra left on the carpet, a vacuum cleaner that looked as if it hadn't been used in a long time, dresses hanging from a wire, children's clothes, a playpen, a few toys, a bottle of tequila, a joint in an ashtray, a canvas spray-painted by a graffiti artist who had run out of walls, and a map of Africa.

"I'll check it out tonight," Roy said.

To kill time, we had a bite at Togo's, a greasy spoon that

served the best soul food in Miami. Fried chicken, yams, bour-bon-flavored plantain.

Night was falling, the sky streaked with large purple stripes. We opened Clean Bug and waited for Acid Profile with an eye on the video clips that were playing on the wide screen. Lita and Roy were warming up the room, which was beginning to fill up with "bugs." I watched Lita dance and regretted having established rules that I wanted to break. She knew it and was playing me like a fiddle.

Even people who didn't know me knew who I was, so that tensions were kept to a minimum. Those who dared hang out in a place like this had better have a good reason, otherwise they were courting suicide. Anyway, I had this particular knack of making friends everywhere I went, as if by magic. I sipped a punch with Jamaican rum and lime and ran Bashma's belongings through my mind. Each one of them was etched on my mental hard drive. I let them float by, waiting on my superprogram to establish connections.

Mona's name came up on my internal monitor. I had to find her; maybe she would have some useful information. Every once in a while Roy would go out to check up on Melody, who was snoozing peacefully on the backseat of the car, wrapped in a blanket.

The club was jammed. Acid Profile finally showed up. He was handsome, six feet four, with a great bod, limber and muscular. He was wearing black silk pants, crocodile ankle boots, a leopard-print shirt, rings on every finger, and a wide-brimmed hat trimmed with a band of fur matching his shirt. He slapped a few hands, sucked on a joint, drained a soda, and nuzzled up to a few cuties who ate him up with their eyes, before climbing onstage. He was so hot that, as soon as he took the mike, the tension shot up in the room to the point where you forgot about your life and your problems and just got high on the music. If, as Gloria said, I was the best fuck on the Gulf of Mexico, this guy Acid Profile had to be number two. His voice stroked each and every girl lined up at the bar; he spoke to them about their bodies, their eyes, rapping wild improvs, and they were flying off their stools. All that was left for him to do when he got offstage was delicately pluck a couple of the most gorgeous ones and take them to his crib to watch the sunrise.

A half hour later he came down to polish off another soda and take the room's temperature. I whispered to him as he strutted by:

"Well done, bro."

"Nothing like the low bass notes to get a pretty pussy wet."

"I got to have a word with you."

"Come to my place around four A.M., the blue house in front of the 7-Eleven next block. There'll be some action."

We hit hands. I stuck around until midnight while the Crew was getting off on the dance floor. I swallowed a few hot sausages brought by the barmaid, danced with a black beauty, blacker than a Jim Thompson thriller, offered her some champagne, tasted her lips, shaped for interminable kisses, and split with my Crew to check out if things were chilling at Rap Monster.

The rap was live, the customers younger; half of them looked as if they didn't even have their driver's license. It was open-mike night; the rap went from worst to def. Each had ten minutes to express him- or herself, unless the audience asked for more. Roy got onstage. He did okay, but he wasn't ready yet. Anything went, from political tirades to instructions on how to steal a car to incitations to debauchery that no radio station would have broadcast. The language was hard, on the beat, without frills; it cut right through the heart of the matter like a razor blade. Meanwhile, Lita was working the room. She was good at picking up useful information. I did the same. People were wondering why Bashma hadn't shown up yet.

A little before three, we got a tip about Mona's whereabouts. We dropped Roy off near the floating market with a poke of dollar bills and headed for the Club, where I was to meet Brad and Joe.

As far as I was concerned, the meeting was going to be short and sweet because I didn't want to miss my date with Mr. Sex and I still had to look for Mona.

Lita popped Salt-N-Pepa's "I'll Take Your Man" in the Beemer's sound system, making the night crackle. Three cheers for the girls of rap. On the way past the airport I saw dozens of cars parked on a service road along the highway. A lovers' lane. Maybe they got a hard-on just watching the planes take off.

The Club was housed in a pretty villa in Coconut Grove. The manager was a friend, Jill. A sweet and funny girl who was pushing three hundred pounds and moonlighted as a caterer of fine dinner parties a cut above what most restaurants served. The Club itself only counted three members, Brad, the chief honcho of the Miami police department; Joe, assistant DA, Dade County; and yours truly. We went to Yale together, where we had founded the Club in direct protest to the stupidity of the endemic brotherhoods and sisterhoods, with the express mandate to explore unknown avenues in Fuck City and the ultimate goal of taking maximum and supreme power.

Brad had a Ph.D. in criminology and was a determined and brilliant politician. It had taken him barely ten years to climb up the ladder of the Miami police department. He was an ace cop, brave and efficient. He had masterminded one of the biggest drug busts in the history of Miami police. He was married, had two daughters, and only got high in the context of the Club.

Joe was the brain. A Ph.D. in law and in political science, he had powerful connections. His father was a U.S. senator. He was in line to be the next DA. He was single but was planning on getting married to further his political career. His only problem was his sexual obsession. He loved violence. Brad and I had more than once pulled him out of a mess. To be honest, he did the same for us and together we liked to think we were heading straight for top success.

We took thirty minutes to talk shop and settle old business before entering Ali Baba's cavern, the sanctum sanctorum where our Jill had prepared a supper of shank of lamb with algae, goat cheese, and raspberries served by ravishing creatures (we called them the icing on the cake). Her menus were simple but each dish was sublime. Since Joe had brought the girls, they were of the hurt-me-darling type, all leather and studs, not exactly my cup of tea. Joe was so hot just imagining the upcoming festivities that his glasses were getting steamed. He was small, squat, fast on his feet. He had been the one to introduce French boxing to the Club. A black belt in karate, he got beat up at Yale—in front of a stunned audience—by a gorgeous French coed who not only was one of the best fucks on campus, a multiorgasmic of the kind American magazines dream about, but on top of that practiced the art of French boxing. She was also very active with women's lib.

After that, for seven years Brad spent his summers in Paris to practice boxing and had made amazing progress in the art. After which he turned us on to it, and as soon as the Club could afford it, we imported Roger, a grand master, and set him up in a converted movie theater, where he worked us out three times a week. We handled student enrollment and before you knew it Roger was driving a convertible Jaguar coupe. But the sport's ultimate refinements he shared only with us, so that we were sure to keep our competitive edge. In retaliation, the kung fu adepts had hired their own master from Hong Kong, but he had promptly been expedited straight to the hospital by our Camembert eater.

True to his calling, Joe had a politician's weasel face, although not without its charm. He was always on edge and pale, on account of his sordid nights, but as sharp as a squad of 170 IQs. He ran around till the wee hours, slept three hours a night, worked fourteen hours a day, was obsessed with butter-flies, and had the intuition of a Cuban Santería card reader.

Brad looked as if he had crawled out of an alligator egg. He was tall and fat, Cuban on his mother's side. He knew all the Cuban curses, had been a swimming champion, and had the quiet look of the sharp-toothed animal who patiently waits on his sandbank for his potential victim to make the slightest mis-take. When he finally made his move, his strike was neat and flawless. In order to get ahead so fast, he had to have killed his way to the top. Nobody had ever seen him angry, which is unusual for a cop. Rumor had it that some of his colleagues had chosen to move out of state rather than end up in a diving accident.

Before leaving the meeting I loaded up on reading mate-rial from Jill's library. A regular insomniac, she devoured a couple of books every night. She let me borrow half a dozen novels, hugging me against her huge boobs. She checked up on Joe to make sure that he was respecting the Club's implicit rules and regulations before settling down with Brad in front of a 1920 Armagnac. I turned down a glass myself: the night was still young for me.

I found Lita smoking a joint in the car, listening to Queen Latifah. She had dropped off Melody at the studio of her sister, a crazed painter who claimed she could only work at night, inspired by the spirit of a Tibetan lama who guided her brush. The sister said she operated in the fourth dimension, and the result of that spiritual symbiosis—sinister creatures endowed with long, hanging tongues—had hit the bull's-eye with the New York art critic establishment. Her monsters were going for twelve thousand dollars a pop. A certified weirdo, she spoke in tongues, which she insisted was an ancient Tibetan dialect of the pre-Christian era, but that even the Dalai Lama would have failed to understand. In short, if she hadn't been an established artist, she would have worn a straitjacket. Melody had probably seen worse.

"How goes the Honorable Society?" Lita asked.

"Not too bad."

"If you let me suck your tongue, I'll tell you what you ate."

I let myself be seduced into a suave nighter. Some nights are made to break rules. And that particular breathless kiss brought back old memories of my acrobatic and lyrical adolescence, triggering positive ions that twirled around in my brain. I felt in tip-top shape. We were only ten minutes late. Amazingly enough, there actually was a blue house across the street from the 7-Eleven.

The vegetation in the yard was so thick one would have needed a machete to cut through it. I could hear Sarah Vaughan whispering "The Island," accompanied by the crickets and all the bugs who must have been getting high in the jungle. The house was rotting; a naked girl swung in a hammock on the deck, catching her breath. The sweet perfume of marijuana welcomed us. The door was open and in the middle of the living room, on a bed round and pink like that of Jayne Mansfield, Acid Profile was playing snake with three foxy ladies. We watched them from a collapsed sofa without interrupting the show, which ended in a complex configuration worthy of Alvin Ailey's choreography.

Acid Profile gently emerged, glowing and relaxed.

"Wow!" Lita commented.

"It's important to live in harmony with nature," Acid Profile said.

"Do you know about Bashma?"

"Yeah, I know . . ."

"Do you know how it happened?"

"The only thing I can tell you is this . . ."

Acid Profile pulled out a .38 with a chrome barrel from under his pillow and blew out his brains.

3

Roy was waiting for us in the car. He was dozing off in the company of a vacuum cleaner, an African mask, a Japanese clock, a set of drums, a mythology dictionary, and a duffel bag full of odds and ends. He opened one blissful eye. Lita was crying. I caught my breath while the half-naked nymphettes vanished into the sultry night.

"Acid Profile's orgasm is pretty noisy," Roy noticed.

"Shut up," Lita growled.

I slid behind the wheel and drove slowly. The night smelled tropical, but the heavy silence warned me that the road would be long and arduous.

Still, I congratulated Roy on his finds. I stopped at a gas station, bought three coffees, some nuts, and a few Milky Ways,

and headed toward Poinsettia Lane, where I had been told I
could find Mona.

The lane was lined with old mango trees, the reason the
area was known as the Fruit Market. "Young love for sale," as
Billie Holiday's song goes. Business was booming: About thirty
hookers, their pimps stationed in Cadillacs and Lincolns, were
surrounded by an army of johns. The girls worked outside or in
the cars. I parked the BMW and took a stroll under the mango
trees. One of the girls came up to me:

"Wanna relax, honey?"

"Yeah, but I'm looking for Mona . . ."

"My tongue is every bit as good as hers . . ."

"I don't doubt it, but she's my girl . . ."

"Over there, see her in the black leather miniskirt . . . ?"

I walked on, lighting my cigar. A group of young dealers
were working the corner. A pimp dripping with gold chains, a
long scar running up his cheek and through his left eye, looked
at me ominously, pulling on a joint bigger than a Churchill.

"If you don't care for hair, I have smooth pussy, but it's
going to cost you more."

"Thanks, bro, I'll keep it in mind."

I finally got to Mona. Believe me, she didn't look like a
schoolgirl, with her black lace bra and the knotted gold chain
hanging between her tits. A regular fantasy machine. If you knew
how to push the right button . . .

She smelled of cinnamon, scanning me up and down
with eyes that had seen more than their share. She looked game.
With her face, her posture, her dark silhouette against the night
sky, her huge eyes glowing in the dark, the rose pinned in her
braided hair, her mouth half-open showing small, pointy teeth,
she barely had to dangle the bait. Two things were immediately
obvious to both of us: One, I wasn't the type to pay her simply

to have a conversation with me in the dark, and two, she wasn't about to hire me to find out who had killed her sister. Life is tough.

"I am a friend of Bashma's."

"She's dead."

"I know. She called me for help."

"Who are you?"

"My name is Zulu . . ."

"Zulu, if you don't mind, let's get out of this hellhole."

I made a sign and Lita rolled up near us. Mona climbed in next to Roy.

At dawn, Miami finally quiets down. Live Crew deserved a little rest. Every night, I decided on my crib at the last minute. I couldn't stand sleeping two nights in a row in the same place. I made a couple of phone calls. I knew all the hotel night clerks and booked a room in one of the art deco hotels on South Beach.

Mona took a shower, and we drank a split of champagne as the ocean liners glided on the horizon in the rising light. She was naked and didn't talk. She put her rose in a glass and watched the ocean. Roy's finds were spread on the peach-colored carpet. I took a shower too. When I came out, Mona had slipped between the sheets. I lay down next to her. She snuggled up to me. I stroked her hair. She cried gently until the street became alive. Then we fell asleep in each other's arms.

We woke up the next day at three P.M. She sat up on the bed with a big smile.

"I'm finished with the tears. Come on, let's have some fun."

I kissed her forehead.

"We've got to talk first."

"Not before putting some pancakes in my stomach."

There's something hilarious about a guy coming out of

a hotel laden with a vacuum cleaner, a clock, and an African mask. The doorman, seeing my predicament, lent me a tote bag; it was more discreet. Mona carried the dictionary.

At the Palace, Gloria gave me an ironical smile. She was a little mad at me for not making good on my promise, but she knew time was on her side. She brought me my mail. Credit card statements, an invite to a new club, Concrete Ecstasy, and a note from my insurance company offering me life insurance.

Mona drained three glasses of orange juice, a pot of coffee, and gulped down two orders of pancakes with bacon. She watched the ocean, her face peaceful.

I had my usual yogurt-fruit-muffin. Mona was a slow starter, like me. She was biding her time, eyeing a fashion magazine that a girl was leafing through in front of us.

"Why are you working on Bashma's case?"

"Because I'm a big fan of her music."

The cellular phone whistled.

"It's George, from the lab. We didn't find anything. The doll was super clean."

"No trace of unusual substances?"

"Nothing."

"So, what's your conclusion?"

"Open-and-shut case. Nothing to say. Natural death."

I didn't believe a word of it, but the advantage of a closed case was that it appeased anxieties and gave me a free hand. No investigation, no suspect. For the cops, at least.

"Shall we take a walk along the ocean?"

"Great idea."

I left the vacuum cleaner with Gloria, after removing the dust bag.

"Are you thinking of going into the housecleaning business?"

"Yes, but without the vacuum cleaner."

"I'm giving you three days to respond to my offer."

"I'll keep it in mind."

I kissed her on the lips.

I took Mona by the hand. We walked on the beach, right at the edge of the waves. Perched on their high towers, the lifeguards behind their tinted windows were watching the fearless swimmers or following topless girls with their binoculars.

After Ocean Drive, where the models, the photographers, and the fashionable tourists hung out, we passed a gorgeous art deco building, the Saint-Moritz, then the Delano, the Ritz, the Marseille, and the Shelbourne, all tastefully renovated by Miami architects. A little further, the beach at the Holiday Inn was swarming with pink bodies. Then it quieted down. Fishermen angled with Cuban rods, a simple line rolled on a plastic reel, with a leader and two hooks. You threw it like a sling, whirling it. The Cubans baited with squid or shrimp. A few snobs cast with spoons and spinners, a more sophisticated technique, but they weren't getting any bites.

There was a clock on the front of the Seville building, a convenient way to tell the time from the beach. The waves brought some jellyfish, seaweed, and sugarcane sticks. Mona was beginning to relax. She watched the ocean liners, the pelicans, the sea gulls, and the sandpipers, which ran so fast on the sand that you couldn't even see their legs move.

"Were you very close to Bashma?" I asked.

"I went to her concerts. Sometimes we'd go out together when she was fucking a rich guy."

"Didn't she make a lot of money? *Felony* sold more than a million copies."

"She had a lousy contract. Sometimes I had the feeling I made more money than she did. She didn't spend very much. Only for her sound system, and I think she put a little money aside for Melody."

"Do you have any idea why they cleaned out her place?"

"Beats me . . . Never heard of anything like that."

"Who would have wanted to kill her?"

"Not the gangs. They loved her. She came out of hell, like them."

"What did she do before she started to rap?"

"Same as me."

"Her ex-pimp?"

"He had his throat slit a long time ago."

"Did Bashma write her own lyrics?"

"When you've gone through what she's gone through, you have enough to say for three lives. That's what rap is all about."

"Do you know her producer?"

"I saw him once. They call him Mono, he lost an eye in Vietnam. He is the owner of Rapadise Records. I think he really liked her."

"What about Acid Profile?"

"His moms must have soaked his cock in a jar of jalapeño peppers. Bashma got tired of him. She dumped him a couple of weeks ago."

"Did she get laid a lot?"

"You know how it is, you throw a party with cool people, and after the squares leave, it often ends up in Amtrak."

"Ever seen anybody who wasn't part of the usual circle?"

"No, some new sisters once in a while, but the core was stable . . . But I heard the cops said it was natural causes."

"So why would she call and tell me: 'They're trying to do me in'?"

"I don't get it. If she had been scared she would have talked to me."

"Did she have friends in her building?"

"They were all her friends."

"What about Acid Profile? Is he the type to kill himself out of love?"

"He killed himself?"

"He shot himself right in front of me. Cool. Just like that."

"I can't believe it."

"I saw it happen. What kind of people did he hang out with?"

"Chicks, mostly."

"And apart from music, what was he into?"

"Sex."

"Did Bashma speak a lot about mythology?"

"Once in a while. She had read a book that turned her on. She lent it to me. The writer explained that male gods were a recent invention. Before that, for millions of years, apparently gods were women."

"I wouldn't be surprised. Was Bashma religious?"

"No, but she liked the idea. When we were kids we used to sing gospel, like everybody else."

"Did you attend the taping of her new album, the one that's due to come out in a few months?"

"No. Mono produced it. She really believed in it. She said it was pure steel. Which is actually the title."

"I've got to listen to it. Do you know where Mono lives?"

"No."

I called the car. Lita answered. They were at the Palace.

"Has Roy finished his waffles?"

"We're ready."

"Drive up Collins, to Eighty-second Street."

Mona peeled off her skirt and T-shirt. She dove headfirst into the ocean and came out laughing like a child. She put her clothes back on her wet body.

"What time do you start work?"

"About ten. Speed isn't too uptight about schedules as long as the cash is there in the morning."

"What's his cut?"

"Fifty-fifty. He's a good pimp."

Mono's production company was located in an old Chinese warehouse. You could still get a noseful of rotten eggs and various Middle Empire delicacies when you walked in. Mono owned a white Mercedes, a black headband, a white secretary, a black desk, a white suit, a black tie, and white gloves. He hated any physical contact. He was a big-time phobic. He had an ugly puss, stunk of money, and thought he was God. Nobody other than him knew anything about rap. Of course, he realized he had just lost his number one star. His desk was cluttered with tapes that hopeful kids unloaded by the wagonful.

"I have exactly three minutes to give you."

I wasn't thrilled with his opening line.

"Listen, black and white, I don't like your attitude. If you don't change it, you're going to find yourself in the mother of all shit storms."

He flashed me a contemptuous smile.

"Nobody weathers shit like I do. Don't be trying to push me, or you'll soon be wishing you never met me."

"We'll see about that."

"You have two and a half minutes left."

"I want to hear Princess Bashma's new CD."

"You might as well ask for the moon."

I told him he had 120 seconds to think about it.

He whistled, and two rattlesnakes slithered into the room, the species that don't shake their tails.

"Throw this punk in the garbage."

I remembered once reading an essay on deconstructionism. A bit boring but the point of it was crystal clear. It was all about the return to primal unity, and because there were two of these guys, I decided to put them back together into one. In less than twenty seconds, the snakes lay under what had been the desk. Mono tried to use his piece, but it somehow flew out the window.

"This is nothing. Just a little appetizer to open discussion . . . I can put the IRS on your ass, close up your operation, and that's only the beginning."

Mono's chairs were in splinters. He stretched his long arms, and his face split into a smile reminding me of an asthmatic seal. He breathed hard:

"I'm open to discussion but you got to understand, there're always assholes bothering me . . . A guy has to take some precautions."

I gave him a friendly smile.

"I can make a tape for you if you'd care to wait."

"A DAT will be fine."

"Please, follow me."

We walked past a bewildered secretary. At the end of the hallway was a studio equipped with a sampler and all the devices. Master tapes were lined up on metallic shelves. A young guy was editing a tape.

"Pedro, would you make a copy of Princess Bashma's new recording for me."

Pedro got up, looked for the master tape, and made a face.

"I can't find it."

"Find it!"

Pedro went over his shelves with laser eyes. He turned green.

"I don't get it."

"Did you give the key to the studio to anyone?"

"Nobody."

"Shit! What the fuck!?"

Pedro was looking everywhere . . . Nothing . . . The day was turning a bit sour for Mono. He rushed to his secretary's desk.

"Kate, all this confusion is because we can't find the new Bashma."

"A messenger stopped by this morning, to take the tapes to pressing. I thought, considering what had happened, that we were rushing the album into production."

"Fucking A! Is everybody insane or what? Pedro, what about the copy? We always make two master tapes, don't we?"

"He took both; he said there could be a drop."

"Stupid cunt! Call Sugar right now."

Thirty seconds later Sugar was on the speaker phone.

"Sugar, you're a cunt. Since when do you make the decision to start production before talking to me?"

"What are you talking about, Mono?"

"You did send a messenger this morning, right?"

"No, I was about to call you—"

Mono threw the phone against the wall. I tried to calm him down.

"No use flipping out. Whoever stole the master tapes will be coming to you with an offer. We'll get them back."

"You better believe it. The motherfuckers are already dead."

"Did you produce the album?"

"Yeah. It's her best, man. We have a shot at the Grammys with it, which means a pile of dough."

"What about the lyrics?"

"The lyrics? Who gives a shit about lyrics?"

"I do."

"By the way, pardon me for asking, but what have you got to do with this?"

"I'm a PI. I'm investigating Bashma's death, finding out who killed her."

"A PI . . . Are you a black belt in karate?"

"French boxing."

"French . . . Man, I thought all they knew how to do in that fucking country was blowjobs and cooking."

Pedro shyly approached.

"I made a personal copy of Bashma's tape, if you want to listen to it. It's in my car."

"Attaboy!"

"If only you had thought to make a DAT, we wouldn't be in this mess."

Pedro copied the tape for me. Mono fired his secretary, and I went to get Melody before locking myself up for a few hours to think.

The kid was fine. She had made good use of the colors and brushes. She had painted a pink house, green palm trees, silver airplanes, and something more abstract, a kind of black scribble on a blue background. Mona said her aunt would take care of Melody. That sounded good to me. I drove the family back to Paradise City. I needed a little solitude to listen to Bashma's three records. Maybe there was something sussable in there.

I booked a room at the Imperial Hotel on Ocean Drive. Ocean view, perfect service, fan, and comfortable bed. Once in my room, I listened to *Felony.* Lying on the bed, I took a pad, a pencil, and called room service for a bottle of Chablis, a chicken salad, and raspberries. The Imperial Hotel had one of the best restaurants in Miami.

Princess Bashma's voice smacked me in the guts. It talked to me and I listened. I wasn't hearing the music, only the lyrics. The bag from the vacuum cleaner was in the corner—I planned to check it out later—and if I found myself in need of something to read in order to fall asleep, I had enough books. But I had another brainstorm. Not all goddesses are found in books. I had a few phone numbers in my pocket.

I had ten seconds' intermission between each cut to swallow a forkful of salad and sip some Chablis. I had that feeling of peace I always experience before a lead or a good fuck. I hoped the lead would come first.

Fifty-two minutes later I had fine-combed *Felony*. Rap's usual themes, the personal style, the voice, the anger had assured the album success. I took a fifteen-minute break. I had noted words, sentences, but nothing had triggered the tiniest light so far.

In *Serious Tits*, the message was clearly less social and more sexual. One of the titles was "Triple X Is My Code." The CD was barred with a black stripe, warning the audience about the obscenity of some of the lyrics. A good advertising coup from that old fox Mono. Actually, the album was so arousing that I could barely hold myself from calling Emergency Services.

The mythological message was clear in *Pure Steel*. Back to Africa, to the dawn of time when woman was Goddess. All of that fitted Princess Bashma to a *T* and I didn't see what would have prevented her from being a goddess. Personally, I would have loved to offer myself in sacrifice on the altar of her body and stick my devotion into her chalice in order to reach perfect communion. The album had everything to become a hit. Whose interest was it to keep it from reaching the public? I had no particular sympathy for Mono, but if someone needed this album and Bashma, it was him.

I assumed that all of Bashma's earnings must have gone into his pocket thanks to a rotten contract, but there were a few details that needed to be checked out before I settled on that conclusion. I examined the articles Roy had found. I took apart the Japanese clock and found what one usually finds in the belly of timepieces. The face was decorated with the image of a geisha holding a parasol, very banal. The batteries were dead. The African mask represented a woman's face, expressive and beautiful. It looked a little like Bashma.

In the bag I found some cheap jewelry, a makeup kit, a photo of Acid Profile, a bottle of nail polish, a joint of marijuana in a matchbox, a beauty salon business card, and a yellow page ripped from a phone book with a listing of photo labs, one of which was circled. As to the contents of the vacuum cleaner bag, I found, in the middle of a lot of dust: a dime, a dead cockroach, remnants of a joint, some dried strawberry jam, probably spilled by Melody, some nail clippings, a movie theater stub, a lock of hair, and a long strand of magnetic tape that probably came from a cassette. I carefully rewound the tape onto a blank cassette and called Roy, who must have been asleep in my car.

"Hi," I said, "this is TWA, we are trying to reduce your wait . . ."

Roy, too, knew how to make music. His specialty seemed to be a kind of synthetic Vivaldi.

"Where are you?"

"Downstairs, just a block away."

"We're going for a ride."

"Can't even take a nap without interruption!"

I found the name and address of Kate Henning, Mono's ex-secretary, on the car computer. I called her up. She was watching TV and said she needed ten minutes to pull herself together. We drove very slowly, and Roy took the opportunity to confide in me.

"No sex between us, do you really mean that?"

"Between who and who?"

"Lita and me . . ."

I looked at him. "If it doesn't interfere with your work . . ."

"Great!"

"Are you on the make?"

"While you were listening to Bashma we played chop-pers."

"Was it good?"

"Far out. Her pussy is juicier than a chocolate softee."

"You still better be keeping an eye on my car."

"We did it right here in the back, man. If the car went, we were going with it. I have been dreaming about her every night for ten days . . . I told her that, she French-kissed me to death, then she did the boogie-woogie . . . Where are we going?"

"To see Kate, Mono's secretary."

"I thought he fired her."

"All the better for us. She'll be more understanding."

I parked the car in front of the Latin Quarter, a new building on Collins Avenue, and rang a bell. She buzzed me in and I rode the elevator up to the tenth floor. She lived in a studio with a stunning view over downtown.

Kate was wearing a shimmering night blue robe like a fifties movie star's. She glittered like the Miami skyline. The studio had a little kitchenette with a bar. On the wall hung a poster of Clark Gable sitting behind the steering wheel of a white sports car. There was a bouquet of red roses on the table, a rack filled with CDs, a wide-screen TV with a large collection of videotapes, and a white leather couch with matching armchair in the art deco style. Everything was in perfect order. The decor was a bit up-tight, but for Kate it must have been a place where she could relax after a day spent with Mono and his crazy goons. I sat down in the leather chair.

"Thank you for letting me in so late . . ."

"What do you drink . . . ? Champagne . . . Scotch . . . mango juice?"

I chose champagne, hoping that she would join me and that it would loosen her up.

"Great view . . ."

"By day, I'd prefer to have the ocean view, but at night the ocean is only a black hole."

She pulled out champagne flutes, skillfully uncorked the bottle, put a Frank Sinatra album on the stereo, and lit a candle, dimming the lights. It was what American women call sensual atmosphere. Personally, it gave me the creeps, but I wasn't in the business of selling Durex condoms. Kate had a body built by aerobics. Everything tightens, including the face, and you think you've gotten rid of your stress. She was a pretty brunet but she seemed too organized and together, like someone for whom life had to be mastered, controlled, everything fitting into a preconceived mold. She must have been a perfect secretary, a lover who had memorized the how-to manual, handing you the certificate of guarantee before you even touched her lips, not to mention that she was probably following some fashionable therapy.

"Don't worry about me. I think Mono is going to take me back. I know how to make myself indispensable. He has a lousy temper, but tomorrow morning he's going to call me screaming, asking me how come I'm not at work . . . But I have to admit, I really did fuck up with those master tapes . . ."

"They're going to show up sooner or later."

She flashed an appreciative smile:

"You did quite a number on Mono's henchmen . . ."

"I don't like violence; the sooner it's done, the better."

"What's your martial art?"

"French boxing."

"Wow . . . I didn't know the French boxed. Very efficient . . ."

"How long have you been working for Mono?"

"A little more than four years."

"What is he like?"

"He's got a great ear, great instinct. He rarely makes
mistakes and since he can't afford to sink a fortune into advertising, he's got to pick first-rate people. Of course, he can fuck up
like everybody else. But look at Bashma, the first album did well,
the second one went Top Seven, and *Pure Steel* is going to be a
megahit. And all that without a big investment."

"Did you know Bashma well?"

"We used to go out once in a while. She was always
friendly, even after she had made it. When she came down to the
office, she'd take me out for a drink. We would chat."

"She seemed to live modestly. A small apartment, no
luxury car, nothing out of the ordinary. Did she make a lot of
money?"

"I shouldn't tell you. If Mono takes me back . . ."

I looked at the bottle of champagne. It was time for a
refill.

"It's very good champagne . . ."

"It's French. It's the only drink I like, so I get the best."

"Would you say that Mono is honest?"

"More or less. I mean, he takes care of himself first, like
everybody else, but he has his moments of generosity. Last
Christmas he gave me a thousand-dollar bonus, just like that."

"The musicians don't have to run after their royalties?"

"You know how it is, they always need advances, but
Mono is pretty decent if the records are selling."

"Why does he need bodyguards?"

"Gangs have tried to put the arm on him. Mono didn't

want to give them more than ten percent. If you pay one gang, all the others come to get their cut. They tell you it's their territory and next thing you know you're in deep shit. Things have calmed down a bit now."

"Have you ever been to Bashma's?"

"Yeah, she threw a lot of parties."

"Amtrak?"

"Not for me, thank you. There are too many viruses around."

Another round and the bottle of champagne was almost finished. We touched glasses gazing deep into each other's eyes. I got up, opened the picture window, and watched the lights of the city until Kate joined me.

"Why are you still investigating? The cops have closed the case."

"Let's just say I am stubborn."

"Doesn't surprise me . . . Do you always get what you want?"

"Sometimes more than I bargain for . . ."

"Did anyone ever tell you that you have a kind of animal . . ."

". . . Magnetism. Animal magnetism."

"So you've heard it before . . ."

"Does your computer have an access code?"

"Do you mean my office computer?"

I smiled at her, drew her to me, stroked her hair, and nodded yes.

"Yes . . . ," she whispered.

Her breathing was coming faster.

"Let me try to guess . . . ?"

Kate giggled nervously.

"It's impossible . . ."

"Did you pick it yourself?"

"Yes."

"You want to play?"

Her breathing really became gasping.

"I don't know."

I kissed her hard, sliding the kiss to the corner of her mouth, stroking her neck at the same time. Her body pressed against mine. I brushed her ear with my lips.

"Tell me just the first letter . . ."

"*P* . . ."

"Is it the name of a band?"

"No . . ."

"The name of a man?"

"No . . ."

"The name of a body part?"

She hesitated a split second.

"No!"

The phone rang. She seemed surprised by it, but answered anyway. I heard her side of the conversation although she was trying to keep her voice low.

"I won't do it again . . . I am sorry . . . It's not a question of money . . ."

She started to cry.

"Give me a chance . . ."

She looked dejectedly at the receiver. The other party must have hung up.

"Bastard!" she screamed.

She wanted more champagne, realized the bottle was empty, went to get another one from the refrigerator, and came back holding the split with one hand, her empty glass in the other. I filled it.

"The bastard really did fire me! He's a real motherfucker.

And decent, on top of that! He's offering me fifteen thousand dollars severence pay!"

Mono had played my hand. I just had to repeat the same questions to get my answers.

I took another chance on the code.

"Physical!"

Bull's-eye!

"Wow! You are unbelievable!"

Now I was going to make Kate relax a little bit. I took her in my arms, laid her down on the couch, stroked her in order to flood her brain with endorphins. Her pupils widened; her body was manufacturing its own drug. The contour of her lips relaxed, just a little.

"You are so gentle," she whispered, before telling me everything I wanted to know.

4

The hangar was quiet. It was almost two A.M. I took a spin around the block, as I always did, to make sure there was no suspicious car. I took my cellular phone with me, left Roy at the wheel with instructions to discreetly cruise the neighborhood, and walked to the headquarters of Rapadise Records. My hyper-alert senses informed me that the honeysuckle was in bloom, that cats were mating, that the moonlight lit up the entire land-scape, and that my path seemed clear. There were other ware-houses around, an old rail track, and in the distance a dog barked.

In the parking lot, a rat jumped out of a trash can, stared at me with bright eyes, and scampered for the gutter. I dialed the code on the bulletproof door and opened the lock with the key

Kate had given me. I didn't lose any time, headed straight for the Macintosh, fed the code to the File Guard. The list of hard-disk files appeared in front of me. I opened the "Sales" file and noted the sales of Princess Bashma's albums. The graphic curve was telling: It climbed straight up. From 12,765 CDs for *Felony* to 797,832 for *Serious Tits.* The other rappers' sales were more modest but there were some hits. Then I opened the "Contracts" file. Bashma got 5 percent of the retail sales price for her first album, 7 percent for her second, 9 percent—that she would never earn—for *Pure Steel.*

It was a standard contract, as far as I could tell, with deductions built in for studio expenses and musicians' fees. Nothing unusual. In the "Royalties" file, I saw that the statements sent to Bashma matched the sales, minus the freebies and the promo copies. With a calculator I added up the numbers and figured out that Bashma had made more than eight hundred thousand dollars in royalties, all paid by checks from Miami City Bank. The dough had to be somewhere.

I came out the same way I got in. Roy picked me up and we headed for Miami Beach. I had to return the keys to Kate. I didn't need to ring the bell. She had also given me the keys to her apartment. She was in bed, the candles still burning. But when I got closer and sat on the edge, I saw the pain that distorted her face. I pulled away the sheet. She was naked. Just as with Bashma, there was no trace of violence. She was dead but nothing seemed to be missing from the apartment. Perhaps I had interrupted the "giver of natural death," as I found myself calling him. I went through the place with a fine-tooth comb.

Kate had supplied me with important information. She knew Bashma very well. There had to be a connection. I called Roy, told him to hide the car, make himself invisible, and let me know if anyone came into the building. In a closet I found a

Polaroid camera and several packs of film. I took photos of Kate, a close-up of her face, her body, and the whole studio. I shuffled through her CDs. Apart from Mono's productions, there was some soul, jazz, and a couple of classics. She had the whole collection of Clint Eastwood movies, some concert videos, a nice selection of Michael Jackson, a few porn cassettes, and a number of musical comedies.

I could easily imagine Mono's rattlesnakes coming for the keys, but in that case they wouldn't have resisted the temptation to intercept me at the warehouse. Something else was bothering me. With one victim and a closed case, the murderer was home free, the cops had thrown in the towel. I was the only one after him. But now, with Kate dead, even the cops were going to wonder.

Kate had a desk. I looked through her papers. Everything was filed: bills, insurance, taxes, garage bills, trips. I wondered where a girl like Kate would travel. There were some plane tickets, hotel and restaurant bills. The tickets had been charged to her American Express card, which gave her an insurance of one hundred thousand dollars in case the plane crashed. She seemed to travel solo. But her destination was always the same: Kingston/Kingston/Kingston.

Always the same hotel, always the same restaurants. I noticed that there were gaps of ten days between arrival and departure for which I couldn't find any bill except taxi receipts of similar amounts, equivalent to ninety dollars. The latest trip was last month.

Kingston is Reggae City, and Rapadise Records' catalog listed some reggae titles. Maybe Kate scouted for Mono. In a closet I found a shoe box full of Polaroids. Family photos, beach scenes, Jamaican landscapes that I put aside, snapshots of men, boat trips, aerobic classes, cocktail parties for the launching of various albums. I recognized most of the catalog's artists. Some of the parties looked as if they had taken place in the Rapadise warehouse, others in a beautiful property surrounded with gardens. Probably Mono's crib. I'd have to get an invitation for a drink. There was a whole series of photos of Bashma taken at one of the parties. I recognized Acid Profile, Mona, Kate, Mono, my main man Stuff, king of hip-hop journalists. He was probably working on his profile of Bashma for *Rolling Stone*. I pocketed the photos that looked interesting. I was thirsty, so I poured myself a big glass of Perrier on ice. I looked through Kate's clothes, smelled her perfume, Opium. I went through her toiletries, her jewelry.

A gold locket caught my attention. It had a sign on it that looked a bit like the infinity symbol, except that one of its loops, bigger than the other, turned into a tail. I remembered seeing a similar piece in Bashma's toilet bag. Maybe they had bought them together. I'd have to put Lita on it. This symbol may have a meaning. A special service in the police archives kept files of signs and symbols. I'd have to wait for office hours to check that out, and also to find out in which bank Bashma kept her money, how much income she had declared on her tax returns, and other significant little details.

But what about Kingston? Before heading there I should talk to Mono about it. I found his private phone number in Kate's Rolodex and I took the whole thing with me. I'd make a copy of it before handing it over to the cops. Kate, being a well-organized girl, had noted the last name, first name, address, and zip code of each and every person. While the phone was ringing, I leafed through the cards and noticed an address in Jamaica.

"Who's the asshole who's calling me in the middle of the night?"

"Who else but your pal Zulu . . ."

"Right! I should have known. What do you want?"

"I'm coming over. I'll be there in ten minutes."

"Can't it wait until tomorrow?"

"No."

"Come on over, then. I sure hope it's worth it."

Kate had an atlas. I found the little town of Black River in the reggae country of Jamaica. Considering its distance from Kingston, I figured it might correspond to the taxi receipts. Another thing to check out. As I gave a last look to Kate, her collection of cassettes caught my attention. I learned a long time ago to trust my instincts. I put the cassettes in my duffel bag.

When I came out, Roy was so carefully hidden that I thought he had split. This kid knew how to melt into the walls, the landscape, under cars. This time I found him comfortably perched in a tree.

The video camera followed us with its eye and the gate opened as if by enchantment.

"I love these swank places. When I break all sales records with my first album, I'll buy a house like this. You'll have your own room."

"Thanks, Roy, you're a pal."

I stopped in front of a majestic veranda. We could have been in Hollywood. One of the rattlesnakes stood outside, a one-man welcoming committee. He wanted to separate me from my gun. I made a sign that I wanted to keep it. He let it go at that.

I walked up a monumental staircase totally devoid of simplicity. The inside of the house was filled with ugly but expensive gadgets that I had already seen in the Polaroids. I walked into the living room. Mono was waiting for me in an English armchair. In his silk robe he looked a little ridiculous.

"You look like Greta Garbo in that getup."

He made a sour face. No sense of humor.

"Stop fooling around and have some coffee."

"I was at Kate's."

"I'm not interested in Kate anymore."

"She's dead."

Mono looked surprised, just the right amount. If he was pretending, he wasn't overacting.

"How's that?"

"Like Bashma."

"It's sort of peculiar, no? As soon as you get close to people, they die of 'natural causes.' "

"I could say the same about you."

"I've seen a lot of things in my life, but this beats them all. Do you think the police department is doing its job?"

"If you knew what they do to corpses, you would avoid dying. They are very thorough. The guys who work in the labs are a totally different breed from the ones who give you parking tickets. Some of them are brilliant and they poke their noses everywhere."

Mono made a vague sign. I pulled out Kate's locket and handed it to him.

"Have you ever seen this?"

"What is it?"

"Some kind of a sign . . . Bashma had the same . . ."

"A sign of what?"

"That's what I'm trying to find out."

Mono emptied his coffee cup. I did the same. It was an excellent mocha from Ethiopia.

"You want to know what I think, Zulu? I think you're torturing your brain too much. I don't see why you're so hung up on this case. Drop it, like the cops did. Who's paying you?"

"It's a secret."

"One of these days, you're going to find yourself dead of natural causes."

"It's going to happen to all of us."

"The later the better for me."

"Do you have any idea what Bashma did with her dough?"

"I don't have a fucking idea. I paid her, if that's what you're implying."

"Did she make a lot of money?"

"Damn right!"

"How much, *más o menos*?"

Mono started to laugh.

"You are un-fucking-believable . . . Just because you've got a detective license, you expect people to tell you all about their private lives."

"None of this is private. If everything is clean, the IRS must know how much you paid her and how much she declared, and if the IRS knows that, I can find out in a few hours. I just want you to save me the trouble."

"You have friends everywhere . . ."

"That's what an Ivy League education is for."

"I believe she must have made between seven hundred thousand and one million dollars in royalties, plus her ASCAP rights. Anyway, you get the picture. Enough jack to buy herself a brand-new car if she wanted."

"Do you think Acid Profile was the type to help himself to her dough?"

"He's not interested in money."

Mono didn't seem to know about his suicide. He also seemed to be playing straight. As far as I could tell, anyway.

"Okay, I am going to let you go back to sleep."

"May I ask you for a favor?"

"What's that?"

"About Kate, I'd rather that the cops didn't know that I had just fired her."

"Sure thing."

"I'll owe it to you."

"It's a free gift, as they say on TV."

Mono got up, slapped my back. It felt as if he had stabbed me. When I got back to the car, I found Roy asleep. I started the car and drove through the gardens. The gate opened and closed behind me. I thought it was weird that a phobic would slap you on the back.

I stopped in a quiet place for a quick nap. Fifteen minutes would do me good—the day had been long and the night was still young.

I felt better as soon as I hit the freeway on my way to Paradise City. Before I got to the Fruit Market, I drove past a gorgeous yellow rosebush. I picked its most beautiful flower, cutting it with the knife I carry along my right tibia, and carefully laid it on the leather seat. Roy was snoring, wrapped up in the white wool blanket. His baby face was moving and I understood why Lita had fallen for it.

I joined the file of cars that were slowly driving past the mango trees. The same pimps were guarding the same street corners. I pulled up next to Mona. As soon as she saw the BMW she ran to me and jumped in. I barely had time to save the rose.

"Zulu, it's dope that you came by!"

She had a fabulously sexy smile. I slipped the fresh rose in her hair. The guy behind me hit his horn. I moved on, passed the slow-moving line. Mona made me pull alongside a huge Lincoln.

She got out to give her pimp his cut and we took off. She

was hungry. I took her to a chic little restaurant in Coconut Grove that stayed open till five A.M. She asked me to choose for her. I ordered a lobster à la nage, a duck à l'orange (the chef's specialty), and a lemon pie (the pastry chef's specialty).

"Killed anybody today?"

"No."

I showed her the locket.

"It's pretty. It was Bashma's . . ."

"Do you know where it's from?"

"No idea. I don't care, as long as it's hers."

"Do you know a girl called Kate, who works for Mono?"

"She's a friend of Bashma's. I've never met her. They used to hang out in the airport's shops together. I think they also went to Kingston to get high."

"The airport's shops?"

"Yo, why not?"

"There's nothing to buy there. Just T-shirts and some tourist shit."

"Maybe, but Bashma always liked planes. Her first boyfriend was a pilot, she used to go wait for him. Maybe it brought back memories."

"Maybe."

I found this tidbit interesting, because of its apparent inanity, so to speak. I was getting tired of all this thinking, and I concentrated on Mona's beautiful allure. She was surprised by the food. She called the maître d' to tell him the cook had fucked up and dropped a jar of orange marmalade on the duck by mistake.

I took the Polaroids out of my pocket. I thought I had seen a picture of Kate and Bashma sitting on seats that could be airport seats. I quickly found it. In the background, a steward was reading a magazine.

"You know, Mona, there must be a bundle of dough for you somewhere. I'll find out exactly how much tomorrow. Not to mention the stolen master tapes of *Pure Steel.* That album should bring you a lot of money."

"It'd be cool to make ten or twenty thou."

"When I say a lot of money, I mean several hundred thousand dollars."

I didn't want to whet her appetite too much. I suspected Bashma not to have been on the up-and-up with her taxes. With all the sensationalistic articles that were bound to come out everywhere, the IRS was sure to get wind of it. Obviously, the master tapes had been stolen for money.

"I'll believe it when I see it."

This kid had a simple and clear attitude in life.

"Do you still have your parents?" I asked.

"My father got killed in a street fight. My mother died of cancer three years ago."

Mona finished her pie. She looked dreamy.

"I need some tenderness," she said with an irresistible smile.

A few minutes later we found ourselves a hotel room.

"You know all the good spots," Mona said, getting undressed.

"I don't sleep very much, so I appreciate comfort."

"What is your home like?"

"I don't have a home. I crash at a friend's pad or in a hotel."

"You're weird . . . Would you come in the shower with me? I like to play with soap."

She didn't have to beg me. The shower stall was big enough for us to lie down on the pink marble under a warm rain. We must have woken up the whole hotel because the phone didn't stop ringing.

The nice thing about luxury hotels is that the hot water never runs out, even after two hours. Mona had a playful instinct, a gentleness, impulses charged with intense emotion, the reflexes of a tigress, a suave and perfumed mouth that felt like a butterfly.

I took her in my arms, carried her to the bed, and finally answered the phone. It was the desk downstairs.

"Sorry to bother you, Mr. Zulu, it seems that screams coming from your bedroom have been heard by several residents . . ."

"Yo, it was only the foreplay. Now we are going to fuck."

"Very well, sir. I will send earplugs up for the other guests."

"Thank you, Paul."

Mona was purring. I brushed her body with my hands, barely touching her, for an hour or two. My fingertips were pulsing, sending out a warmth that went deep into her. Her body undulated, twisted, tightened, stretched, rolled and unrolled. She moaned gently, a deep throaty sound that seemed to come out of each and every one of her pores. Her skin smelled like an exotic fruit. I tenderly licked her nape, her eyes, her face, her neck, slowly spiraling down, exploring each recess of her body. Her underarms and the sides of her breasts were particularly sensitive. The lower the spiral went, the closer she got to orgasm. She came when my tongue traced the line of her left hip. Her whole body started to shake, she screamed and kept twisting like a dancer, offering every part of her to my lips and tongue.

She came another eight or ten times and fell asleep before I could enter her. I realized that with Mona we wouldn't get to the actual lovemaking part unless we had at least a dozen hours ahead of us. I fell asleep dreaming that I had fallen in the middle of a lily.

I woke up in her mouth. I had had a dream that now came back to me bit by bit. The sign on the locket was in flames. Old men dressed in black were looking at it. I was there, observing the scene, hidden in the jungle. There was only one woman; she was a combination of Bashma and Mona. She was frantically dancing in front of the old men.

I told Mona my dream. She was sitting cross-legged in the middle of the bed, eating pancakes with her fingers. The maple syrup was dripping between her breasts. I licked it off, which made her giggle irrepressibly. With Mona, there was no dead time. Even asleep she seemed to eat up life.

It was late. Paths leading to the unknown were opening up before me. I had to follow them. I promised Mona to pick her up early that evening, watched her climb into a cab, and met with Lita and Roy, who were fuming. We had a heavy program.

"Kate Henning is dead. Just like Bashma. Tell Brad: Go to the Latin Quarter on Collins, top floor."

I let Lita handle that.

"Did you sleep well, Roy?"

"I put on a Bruce Springsteen album, put me right to sleep. I ordered breakfast on your account. It's a good place, here. Now I am as cool as a cucumber."

"Lita, check the banks' computers and get the numbers of Bashma's bank accounts."

Lita pulled out her file, dialed her access code. She had written down Bashma's real name: Corlina Lewis. As expected, Bashma had no bank account anywhere, no credit card. Lita checked with the phone company, with Miami Power and Light. Bashma paid everything in cash.

"Roy, would you mind playing *Serious Tits,* fourth cut."

Roy rushed to the trunk, slid in the CD. I fast-forwarded until I got to the part I had registered in a corner of my brain:

Triple X was my code.
High in the sky with my lead
We were flying.

Lita sat behind the wheel.

"To the Palace."

Gloria gave me Bashma's belongings. She reminded me that I had only two days left to give her a call. I dropped the vacuum cleaner bag off at the police lab. At least they couldn't tell me there was no clue. I ran the African mask through the X rays. There was something in the sculpture's interior. The work was so well done, the ebony grain so tight, that it was impossible for the naked eye to discern the simple and perfect mechanism that allowed the removal of the central portion of the skull to reveal, in a tiny cavity, a key to a locker with the number 16. Of course, said locker had to be at the airport.

I found the locker without trouble. I turned the key. I still had to crack the code. *Triple X* had to be translated, since the dial had only numbers. *X* was the twenty-fourth letter of the alphabet and the second one from the end. I tried 2-4-2. The sesame opened. It contained a leather bag. I grabbed the bag, picked up Live Crew, and, while we were driving along the freeway, examined the contents. It was Bashma's bank. There was a lot of money. But there were also a few other interesting objects. Plane tickets to Kingston with the same dates as those I had found at Kate's; a little clay pot, empty, with a sign carved in the clay. It was the same sign as the one on the locket that I had left at police headquarters. I called the technician up. He said he couldn't find anything that matched the sign exactly. The closest connection was a group of communist scientists and artists, the Infinity Movement, who had used a similar symbol during the McCarthy era, but all that was a long time ago, and I didn't see how a group of scientists in the fifties could have any connection with the ghetto today, unless they had invented the ultimate weapon to kill people without a trace. Of all the members of the Infinity Movement, three were still alive. One was a Nobel Prize winner. I wrote down their addresses.

The Nobelist was professor emeritus at Stanford University. The second guy lived in East Hampton, New York, and the third one taught at Columbia University. I had to meet them right away. I managed to talk to two of them on the phone. I made an appointment at Stanford for the following day. I left myself just enough time to get across country back to New York, where I would try to meet with the Columbia professor. I would go out to the Hamptons afterward. Then a little detour through Kingston to listen to some good reggae and visit Kate's friend, whose address I had.

The money would be a nice surprise for Mona, enough to get by for a while. I checked the IRS files. Bashma had never declared more than sixteen thousand dollars' income a year. You couldn't tell she made more by examining her life-style. On the other hand, if Mono was audited, they would catch her. I had to find a good lawyer to arrange for a voluntary declaration by Mona to avoid paying a fine, or any criminal charges against Bashma's estate.

I had a safe-deposit box in my bank, since I didn't get all my money paid by checks either, so I put Mona's dough in the vault. I kept a roll of bills to give Mona. She could do a little shopping with it. The problem was her pimp; he shouldn't get wind of this. But she was a smart kid. She would understand the advantage of being discreet.

The newspapers had started to take an interest in Princess Bashma's mysterious death. Overnight she became the only rapper worth talking about. Mono had to be going crazy. I called him up.

"Yo, Mono, no news of the master tapes?"

"Nada, so far. What about you?"

"I'm making progress . . ."

"These little bastards' days are numbered. Let's keep in touch."

"Okay, ciao. Ah, wait a second . . . I was forgetting . . . Steve Clesh, does it ring a bell?"

"Never heard of him."

I talked with Brad. His department was beginning to ask themselves questions about these two deaths from natural causes. They were panic-stricken, imagining a new weird virus; the state medical authorities were already in on it. This whole thing was quickly turning into science fiction.

I headed for the Fruit Market a lot earlier than usual. Was I getting addicted to it? Maybe. Mona was surprised to see me.

"I still have a long way to go tonight," she told me.

I pulled three hundred dollars from my pocket, handed the wad to Mona. She winked at me and nonchalantly crossed the street toward her pimp's Lincoln. He got out of his car, took the dough, and came up to me.

"Yo, man . . ."

"Yo. You like the kid?"

"Yep."

"You got good taste, but don't be keeping her away from her work. Next time, come around four or five, all right?"

"No problem. I understand the business."

"Better for you."

Mona hopped in the car and kissed me. It gave me shivers all the way down to my toes. It felt as if I'd inhaled a deep hit of pot.

"I got a surprise for you . . ."

"Me too . . ."

"Super . . . Turn left . . . There, straight on . . . Hmmm . . . Something smells good . . ."

"It's you"

"No, it's the jasmine that's in bloom."

"As a matter of fact, you smell of jasmine."

"Really?"

"At the gas station, make a right and stop in front of the little white house, right here . . ."

It was a tiny wooden house that looked all eaten up by the termites. It leaned a little to the right. There was a narrow deck with a beat-up couch, a skeletal palm tree, and a tobacco-colored lawn. The neighborhood was in the same state. The street was full of kids fooling around. On the decks, whole families drank, told stories, everybody was laughing. An old man had pulled out his TV and his skinny silhouette was lit up by the flickering colors on the screen. Down the block, teenagers were dancing in a garage and a dozen Michael Jacksons moon-walked under the admiring eyes of their girls.

"It's a good block. We all know each other."

A rosebush that Mona must have watered every day stretched its beautiful yellow flowers in the night. A delicious smell of barbecue floated in the air.

"It's my home. My house. Come in!"

I waited for her to open the door.

"Come in, it's open. It's not worth spending money on triple locks; the kids around here could slip into Fort Knox. Anyway, the partitions are thinner than paper. I paid eight thousand dollars for it. What do you think? Not bad, huh?"

I walked in. There were three tiny rooms. A living room overlooking the deck, a bedroom on the right, and a kitchen at back. There was a good smell of cooking in the house.

"My aunt made us a pig's tail and ear stew. I hope you like that."

"My folks eat that too. I love it."

I went into the kitchen, picked up the top of the skillet, sniffed. A lot of images shot through my mind. On the fridge was an orange-flower cake, a bottle of cabernet sauvignon, and a bouquet of marigolds.

The windows were covered with curtains of white canvas hung by brass rings. In the living room, the couch was a foam rubber mattress with pillows. There was also an old TV, a stereo, magazines, records, a photo of her parents, another of Bashma. In the bedroom, a big brass bed took up the whole space. A crate with a mirror on it was nailed to the wall so that you could see yourself from the bed. A big gray cat was asleep on the red blanket.

"His name is Drums."

"Hi, Drums . . ."

He couldn't care less about me, but soon he would have to make room for us. Mona set the TV on the floor and pulled the table out on the deck. She wanted to lay a tablecloth on it. Her tablecloth. She put "Round Midnight" on the turntable, played by Wes Montgomery. There was a superb sax solo by Johnny Griffin, an underrated musician. Mona uncorked the wine and poured it. She scooped a big spoonful of white rice into a platter and topped it with a large serving of stew. It was getting a little dark, so she went to get a candle, stuck in a Chianti bottle over which dozens of candles had already dripped.

"It's a good surprise."

Mona had not set silverware. We ate African-style. It was delicious.

"What about *your* surprise?"

I pulled out a wad of bills.

"Here is ten thousand dollars. It's your money, and let me tell you, it's only the tip of the iceberg. I found Bashma's stash in an airport locker."

"Is that where she kept her dough?"

"That's it. And in spite of what you thought, Mono was on the up-and-up with her."

"Cool! I hope you found a better spot for the money."

"It's quietly sleeping at Miami City Bank. We'll open a bank account for you, but before that you'll have to see a lawyer and straighten things out with the IRS. Bashma never declared any income that would have put her into a taxable bracket. I suggest that you spend your money very discreetly."

"Don't worry, I'm not going to buy a Mercedes. This is great."

This turned out to be one of the hottest meals—food- and emotionwise—that I had eaten in years. The orange-flower cake and the strong coffee were divine. We lay down on the couch. Kids were circling the BMW, their eyes lit up like Hallow- een jack-o'-lanterns.

"Can we sit in it, please, mister, please?"

"Yo, go 'head."

In less than two minutes there was a line. The kids got in six by six, screaming crazy comments.

"It's early," Mona said. "You want to go dancing? I know a place."

Before leaving, we had to drive around the block twenty times to satisfy the desires of all the kids who wanted to hear the engine purr.

We were crossing a pretty sleazy avenue. Bums, second- and third-generation whores, crackheads, junkies, and drunks were standing around the liquor stores, bodegas, fast-food joints.

Suddenly, three hundred feet ahead of us, I saw a home- boy spray-painting a white wall. I recognized the sign even before he finished it just because of his arm movements. It was

Bashma's sign, the one on her and Kate's lockets. I slammed on the brakes, swerving the car alongside the curb. The graffiti artist immediately took off, zigzagging like an arrow on PCP through the indifferent zombies, with me following. He ran incredibly fast. No way I could catch up with him. He crossed the street, causing a collision. Running through a bar, we ended up in the backyard. The kid leaped the brick wall like a cat. I split the crotch of my pants. On the next block, I saw him dash into a movie theater. I followed him. The screen was dark; it took me thirty seconds before I could make out the faces in the audience.

Ten minutes later I gave up. The kid had vanished. I walked back to my car. It was rare that someone could outrace me. A group had gathered on the sidewalk. Some mean-looking guys wanted to know what I wanted from the kid. I told them I owned an art gallery and had discovered the next Keith Haring.

We drove on, mulling over our artist and his fixation on the fatal infinity sign. I called up Roy. I had given him the night off. I knew he was with Lita. She picked up the phone.

"Lita, I saw a kid who was spray-painting our sign on a wall on Little Avenue. I ran after him, but he shook me off. I want you guys to try to find him while I interview the communist scientists."

"No problem."

She was very professional.

"Take care of yourselves."

"That's exactly what we're doing, Zulu. Watch out for your own self in Kingston. It's violent over there."

"If all the chicks are like you, they're going to tear me to pieces."

"Gotta hang up, man, you caught us in full motion."

Mona and I danced till dawn, glued to each other, like

layers of fiberglass swaying on an ocean of pure pleasure. Mona was under my skin and it was reciprocal.

After a red-hot night and a change of clothes, I boarded the airplane just as the steward was about to close the door.

5

The shock of the landing woke me up. It was raining over Frisco Bay. I had rented a Porsche. It was black and had that delicious smell of a brand-new car. There were only four miles on the odometer. I had the delicate mission to break it in. My appointment was in twenty minutes. I sped through the pouring rain. John Silverstein had told me to follow the big, palm-treed avenue, which is what I was doing, to make a left three blocks down, and to count five houses. There was no water shortage here. By the time I got under the awning, I was soaked. It was a beautiful brick house, colonial style, with Doric columns. I rang the bell, a musical chime welcomed me, then the door opened and an old woman with a beautiful face and a serene expression appeared.

"My husband is expecting you. What would you like to drink?"

"I'd love some tea."

"Darjeeling, Lapsang souchong, or orange pekoe?"

"Orange pekoe, please."

I saw that she found me charming and well behaved, which made me feel all funny and reminded me of my years at Yale. It was only later that I had adopted this no-frills demeanor. It was the Miami influence.

My Nobel Prize winner got up to shake hands with me. He too had the beautiful face of a Viennese Jew. He must have arrived in 1935, '36. His accent was delicate and full of charm. He invited me to sit in a comfortable chair. The atmosphere was quiet and cozy, the room full of books, and those for which there was no room on the shelves were piled on the edges of a kilim carpet. Silverstein looked sick but his eyes were vibrant, questioning, and bright.

"You wanted to see me about the Infinity Movement?"

"Yes, I am a private detective and I am investigating two strange murders committed in Miami these last few days. A rap singer and her friend have been assassinated by untraceable means. No trace that the autopsies could reveal."

"It's surprising—"

"It seems that the author of these crimes uses a sign that is similar to yours."

I showed him the locket. He took it in his shaking hands, examined it.

"Yes, it's similar, but our movement folded a long time ago and our preoccupations were very far from those you mention."

"I understand, but you know how it is, we mustn't neglect any clue. In my profession one spends a lot of time on false leads . . ."

"It is like scientific research and I myself have found that often major discoveries happen almost by accident."

His wife served us tea.

"I am afraid you came all the way for nothing. I am sorry . . . If you want me to talk about our movement, I'd be glad to. It was a fascinating time and our fight meant something . . . Would you like to stay for lunch? Rachel will prepare us a snack."

I accepted. I liked this couple's company, and if I wasn't going to learn anything about my murders, I would at least discover a page of history.

I took the red-eye back to New York, spent a comfortable night in the first-class cabin, and landed in the Big Apple as fresh as a bottle of champagne. I took a cab to the Plaza. My room overlooked the park and the weather was almost nice. The leaves were coming out; the whole park around the large reservoir was a light green that stood out in the middle of the gray buildings. I settled down in my room. It was a bit early to make phone calls. I took out a novel by Don DeLillo, *White Noise,* and read it in one sitting. It was a wonderful book. I then rang for a solid breakfast and started dialing. My appointment in East Hampton was at six P.M. and my New Yorker, Samuel Parker, was still not answering his phone. He lived on Ninety-second and Broadway.

I decided to walk all the way up this memorable avenue.

I stopped by at Shakespeare & Co. and bought all of DeLillo's novels and slowly strolled on. I stopped by at a boutique called Zone 3, bought a skin-tight dress for Mona, a pair of pants for Lita, and a red leather cap for my favorite rapper. Now it was time to try my luck at Samuel Parker's.

His lobby looked like that of a Babylonian temple. An obese black doorman was reading a Stephen King novel, *The Dark Half.*

"It's one of his best ones, in my opinion . . ."

"Are you a fan?"

"I've read them all. 'George Stark—There are no birds—George Stark'—it's a little further in the chapter you just started, 'Automatic Writing.' "

He turned the pages, got to the sentence written by hand in the book, and looked at me with astonishment.

"Fucking memory you've got!"

"Is Sam here?"

"Samuel Parker?"

"Yes."

"He left about ten minutes ago."

I looked at my watch with surprise.

"I am a bit late. We had an appointment at ten. I'll wait for him."

"Are you family?"

From his question, I assumed that Parker was a cultural megamix like me.

"He is my uncle."

"I think he went to the drugstore on Ninety-sixth Street."

"Thanks. I'll go see if I can find him."

I walked up Broadway, looking into every store. Parker was seventy-eight; I knew he had taught anthropology at Columbia until he retired. I found him in the drugstore. He was buying ginseng and sleeping pills. He was short, skinny, darker than me. He still walked straight and looked relatively alert. I observed him for a minute. His eyes were strange, a bit lost, maybe he had eye problems. I waited for him to pay, walked out of the drugstore ahead of him, took a few steps in the direction of his apartment building, and turned around just in time to come face to face with him.

"Mr. Parker!"

He looked up to me with his lost eyes. I saw that he had trouble placing me.

"It's so nice to see you after all these years! It's incredible, you haven't changed at all since Columbia."

His face lit up with a smile.

"A former student of mine . . ."

"Charles Grove . . . Don't you remember me . . . ?"

"Grove . . . Grove . . . Oh God, I am afraid I am losing my memory . . . Do you live in the neighborhood?"

"I came to buy books at Shakespeare & Co."

"Very good bookstore. I go there too. Grove . . . Grove . . . An anthropology major?"

"No, literature, but I loved your classes."

"Did you come to the Wednesday sessions, at my place?"

"Do you still live on Ninety-second?"

"Yes, but my wife passed away. I am alone now."

"She was so sweet."

Parker's eyes became veiled.

"She passed away three months ago. I don't have the will to live anymore. I don't go out. I don't even answer the phone. Each time I walk across Broadway I wish a cab would run me over. I miss the contact with young people, nobody ever visits me anymore."

"I would love to invite you out for lunch. I am free."

"I'd love to, but I can't stand going to the places Grace and I used to go to. I know all the restaurants around here."

"Let's take a cab to another neighborhood."

"Okay . . . But I wouldn't want to impose . . . You must have more interesting things to do."

I hailed a cab and asked the driver to drive down Broadway.

"What would you like to eat?"

"I don't know . . . Chinese, maybe . . ."

"To the Four Dragons," I told the cabbie, who, according to his ID plate, seemed to be a freshly landed Russian. "On Canal Street."

Parker looked shyly at the street, the buildings, the people on the sidewalks.

"At least the weather is nice. The winter has been terrible. I have my groceries delivered to my apartment so that I won't have to go out. You know, when you look at them closely, people's faces look distorted and the more you stare at them, the more distorted they become. It's better not to look at them too much."

We settled down at a quiet table. Parker wanted dim sum as appetizer, followed by chow mein. I ordered the same for myself and a bottle of California rosé.

The wine made him feel good. He rarely drank. His face became a little more animated.

"What do you do now?"

"This will surprise you. After my B.A. in Spanish literature, I became interested in criminology and I got a Ph.D. from Yale."

"Excellent university . . ."

"Today, I am a private detective."

"Anthropology being the science of man, it makes sense. Do you practice in New York?"

"No, in Miami."

"They say it's a beautiful city, where the Jews go to die."

"It is a beautiful city."

"You know, it's strange, when you don't have the wish to live anymore, the future looks like a field of gray cotton. Everything is gray, but here, in Chinatown, there is a lot of red."

"This is the toughest investigation of my career. The police have thrown in the towel and I am the only one to persist . . . Do you mind if I talk to you about it?"

"No, not at all. You see, I have serious problems with my eyes, so I buy novels taped on cassettes, and the last one I listened to was *My Gun Is Quick,* by Mickey Spillane."

"I like Spillane. He is being rediscovered and people are realizing he wrote a language as hard as the steel barrel of a .38."

We finished our dim sum, drank a little wine before the piping-hot chow mein was brought to the table.

"Smells great," Parker said.

He handled his chopsticks deftly. I told him about the mysterious events, about the sign. He wanted to see the locket. The story captivated him.

"Not a trace . . . not even of those poisons used by certain Amazonian tribes, like the red roots?"

"All of these substances are well known by the labs. Some murderers have used them thinking their crimes would go unpunished, but criminal science has made enormous progress lately."

"What about this little clay jar, do you have it with you?"

I showed him the Polaroid I had taken of it.

"I believe this kind of jar is used by voodoo initiates to store spiritual substance in the form of hair and nail clippings. This ceremony takes place during initiation. The voodoo priest himself cuts the nails and the lock of hair. The jar is then placed near the image of the god to whom the priest is devoted and who gives him his power. In case of the disciple's disobedience, the priest possesses his soul and can act on it."

"And kill it."

"Yes, but in most cases, it wouldn't be an instant death. This kind of malediction brings a slow death. Only an exceptional force can bring instant death . . . Certain voodoo priests, I heard, are capable of doing that with the help of a strange technique . . ."

Parker swallowed a few noodles. He was amused by my surprise.

"They concentrate on a large clay bowl full of water. They invoke their god and bring forth the image of their victim on the surface of the liquid, then, with a dagger, they stab the image. If the procedure is successful, the water turns into blood."

"Did you ever attend such a ceremony?"

"No, these are extremely protected and secret rituals, but I have been able to reconstitute these sessions from various accounts, and certain authors mention them."

"What can one do to protect oneself against such practices?"

"Not a whole lot. The only solution is to enlist the help of a voodoo priest with the power to fight the one who cast the original spell."

"It seems unbelievable . . ."

"I know. We live in a time that has the need to explain everything."

"Even if all this were indeed possible, the voodoo priest would still have to get hold of the nails, the hair—"

"Or a piece of clothing."

"Is it difficult to fight such power, to find someone who would accept to do it?"

"Yes . . . The voodoo priest would first have to assess the strength of the spell. If his opponent is more powerful than he is, he risks death by engaging in such a magical fight. Those who accept to do it charge a lot of money and a lot of them are quacks. Needless to say, a number of slow deaths from illnesses are falsely blamed on voodoo. It is a growth industry, mostly run by Haitians, who are very numerous in New York and in Miami. What I don't understand, in your story, is the motive. Why would a priest put a 'death warrant' on a young singer and her friend?"

"What about the presence of the empty jar in the personal belongings of the singer? What do you make of that?"

"It could mean that the initiate had bought her soul back from its master. It is common practice when an initiate wants to change voodoo priests."

"And the sign?"

"The sign could be derived from the symbol of a god, or maybe of a *humfo,* which is the place where the voodoo priest, also called *hungan* or *hambo,* practices. It is the place where the *loa,* or spirit, possesses him. It might also represent a curled-up snake, a familiar image in voodoo."

"Are you still in contact with hungans?"

"No . . . I stopped working in that field a long time ago, but I know a few people who could help you. It's a strange world, it can be terrifying."

"Could a voodoo priest make a diagnosis from a picture?"

"Of course."

That conversation left me thoughtful. I took Parker back to his apartment, thanked him for his help. He told me my visit had made him feel better. I hoped he would gradually find his zest for life again. He took me up to his apartment, which was a real voodoo museum. I became acquainted with sacred drums and other ritual objects. He offered me one of his books, which was still considered definitive, and the address of a Haitian woman in Harlem who was in contact with the underground world. He also gave me a talisman in a little leather pouch attached to a cord. It had been given to him by a powerful hungan, who had advised him to wear it.

"Take it," he said. "My illness is inside of me but you might need it. Wear it around your neck and never take it off."

I dropped off my packages at the hotel and took a cab

to Harlem. I found myself in front of a bombed-out brick building. Madame Clementine lived on the third floor. Parker had promised he would call and announce my visit to her.

The door was practically off its hinges. It was half-open. I knocked and went in. A dark passage ran along a kitchen in which three cats pushed each other's face to eat from an aluminum bowl. The whole place smelled of cat piss, and when I got to the living room I discovered about twenty felines regally stretched on the couch, the chairs, the windowsills, warming up in the sun. Clementine, a little old woman all withered and chubby, was expecting me, comfortably ensconced in an armchair that seemed to have become permanently attached to her. The mark of the casters on the floor made me realize that she too was following the trajectory of the sun. She looked at me with a penetrating gaze. She didn't smile, but there was a kind of benevolence emanating from her person. She was dressed in bright colors, like a Mexican peasant woman, or a Gypsy. A pineapple and a big kitchen knife were laid on a round wooden board.

"You are a friend of Parker's. A detective . . ."

"Thank you for accepting to see me so soon."

"Seeing people is all I do. So people have died and you don't know why."

"Exactly."

In a corner of the room stood an altar with the image of a voodoo god, burning candles, cigars, and a bottle.

"It's Exu. He likes rum and cigars. He is a very powerful god. Show him your photos."

I took out the Polaroids and put them on the table, as she indicated to me. She looked at them one by one, particularly the one representing the tormented face of Kate.

"It's 'Red Eyes' . . ."

"Who?"

"A very evil spirit, cannibalistic, a devil. Only a very powerful hungan can send that kind of death."

"Is it possible that death comes in a very short time?"

"Yes, sometimes instantly."

"Kate—this young woman—and Bashma were killed instantly."

"Undoubtedly. But hungans capable of performing such *envois-morts* have disappeared with the coming of the city and civilization. I knew one, when I was a girl in Port-au-Prince. Since he died, I have never seen, never heard of a hungan who would still have such power. Was the *pot-tête* empty?"

"Yes, but there were nails and hair clippings in the vacuum cleaner bag."

"Is it possible to find out if the hair and nails belonged to the victim?"

"Yes, the lab can tell me that."

"It is important. Certain initiates buy back their soul and the voodoo priest who introduced them to the gods gives back the *pot-tête,* but sometimes the priest, wishing to keep a disciple in his power, will give him the wrong jar, with nails and hair that don't belong to him. When can you find out?"

"Tomorrow."

Clementine cut two slices of pineapple, peeled off the rind, and gave me a slice. I sunk my teeth in it. A delicious juice ran down my chin.

"Life is pretty good, isn't it?"

"Yes."

"So why do you want to die?"

"I don't want to die. I am not taking any chances. Parker gave me this," I said, showing her the amulet hanging from my neck.

"It's good, but it's not enough."

"I'm not about to give up."

"So you risk ending up like your friends with your face twisted in pain."

"I want to understand."

"One doesn't understand voodoo, one lives with it, or dies from it."

I ate my slice of pineapple and thought about that. I thought of all the bullets that had grazed me, of all the times I had escaped what seemed certain death.

"If such a powerful voodoo priest exists, there's got to be someone who would have the power to oppose him."

Clementine smiled for the first time.

"One progresses in evil faster than in good. Such a person probably exists, but he or she would have to accept a magic fight with a deadly enemy."

"Does it seem unlikely to you?"

"You'd have to find that person first. You are seeking two people who must both be equally hidden, protected. To enter that world is very dangerous, you can lose your mind and your life. No matter what, if you cross the magic circle, pain awaits you."

She cut two more slices of pineapple and stared at me in silence. I looked at the altar, the candles, the rum, the cigars, the colored divinity. I took out the locket and showed it to her.

"They were wearing this sign."

"It's probably the hungan's sign, the sign of his group."

"A snake?"

"No, the snake is positive in voodoo. It is widely used. But hungans who send death fear it and would not choose it as a symbol. It is something else. Maybe knotted intestines."

Clementine's hypothesis seemed quite plausible to me.

"May I come back tomorrow?"

"Whenever you want."

"I'll bring cigars and rum."

"Exu will appreciate this gesture. See you tomorrow, my son."

I walked around Harlem a little, then took a cab back to the hotel. I felt my intestines quiver.

The red light on my phone was blinking, signaling a message. It was from Lita. I called her right back.

"Hiya, beautiful, I bet you are on the beach or in bed with Roy, this poor, pure young man whom you are turning on to the basest debauchery."

"It's serious, Zulu. Melody, Bashma's daughter, has been painting."

"Cool, we'll have to find a gallery for her."

"She begged for paint and brushes, so I took her to my sister's and she's been at work all day. Always painting the same thing, always red . . ."

"The sign?"

"Exactly. You should see her when she paints. Her eyes are terrified, her body is all stiff, as if she was reliving Bashma's death."

"Incredible . . . I'm on to something. It's crazy . . . I am beginning to enter the darkness . . . Real spooky . . ."

"Here, the sky is blue. We would be very sad if you didn't come back."

"Man! You guys are really encouraging . . ."

"Roy says the hip-hop gods will protect you."

"The devil will take it in the ass."

"Yeah. The whole fist."

"Famous last words. Well, back to the coal mines. Wish me luck."

"Gee, that almost sounded like a rap."

"Ciao, gorgeous. Oh, I almost forgot. Call the lab and ask them to check the hair and nail clippings that were found in the vacuum cleaner. See if they're Bashma's."

"Okeydokey, mokey. I'll call you as soon as I have the answer."

I called one of my exes. She ran a limousine service. The float consisted of a stretch Cadillac and herself. She agreed to drive me to East Hampton, where I had to see my last customer.

She was downstairs waiting for me. She was a beautiful brunet, Rita Hayworth style. She had Rita's eyes, her mouth, her bust. As for the rest, I don't know, I never did it with Rita Hayworth.

Her name was Laura Gozzi and she had a stream of lava from the Etna volcano running in her veins. To my surprise, she was not at the wheel. A young guy named Luis was in charge of the technical end of the transportation. Laura and I were going to take care of the other part, in the back, in the company of a bottle of champagne.

"It's good to see you again, Zulu . . ."

"You don't get down to Miami too often."

"How can I? I work eighteen hours a day. I have two limos now, and Luis. Did you rent a house in the Hamptons?"

"No, I am here for work."

Laura closed the opaque glass partition and undressed me with an ardor that reminded me of bygone days. It was a smooth ride. The subtle aroma of her cunt was like a childhood memory. With Laura the nights had always been tropical, full of tears and screams.

When the car pulled to a stop, the silence found us glued to each other, in total bliss. We finally realized we had reached our destination. I reluctantly got back into my clothes. I was completely under Laura's charm. The talisman had not protected me from that spell.

Stewart Nordvensen lived in a splendid white villa, all made of glass, steel, and cement, isolated among the dunes, facing the ocean. The sea air cooled me out as I climbed the stairs of a very pure design. I walked on the terrace. There was no curtain; the inside was wide open, with a few spots of color. No books, no mess, clean as a whistle. A shape was swinging in a hammock. Nordvensen was wrapped in a plaid blanket. His dry face and faded eyes gave him the air of a sailor who'd lost his ship.

"Mr. Nordvensen?"

"Who do you think I am?"

I pulled up a chair of such modern design I had the feeling of sitting on a nail. The old man didn't offer me anything to drink. Obviously I was bothering him.

"I won't keep you long . . ."

"I hope not, I hate cops . . ."

"I understand that you have bad memories, but I am not a cop."

"Same difference. You get paid to make people talk, and I don't like to talk."

I was not going to stick around here too long.

"Don't you read anymore?"

"What's the point of reading when everything has been said and done?"

"Say what?"

"There is only one problem in life."

"Which is?"

"I won't answer that question."

I showed him the locket.

"Have you ever seen this?"

He didn't even look at it.

"No."

"Is the Infinity Movement dead?"

"As dead as that dog McCarthy."

"The infinity sign was badly chosen, then?"

"It's the first intelligent thing you have said so far."

"Watching the ocean all day is not good for you. It turns you nasty."

"I am what I am but at least I know it, which is not your case."

"You are on a slow cycle, but you end up answering my questions one way or another. Do you like rap?"

"Hate it."

I was surprised that hip-hop culture had even reached this deserted place.

"I am thinking of *Moby-Dick,* maybe I am in search of the white whale . . ."

"It's possible."

"Okay, I am not going to bother you any longer. I'm on my way."

Nordvensen didn't respond. From the frozen Antarctic I was heading back to the tropics, but on my way I passed through the inside of his house. Call it intuition. I always follow mine. Intelligence has its limits. In the large living room, I noticed a lighter shape on the white wall. An oval object had been hung there and removed. The ocean light had had the time to draw its outline. Oval . . . Face . . . Mask . . . Why not an African mask? I rummaged through my pockets and in place of the missing object I hung the Polaroid of the mask found at Bashma's. A souvenir for Nordvensen.

By the time we got back to the city, Laura and I were starved. We went to Shennigan, where the steaks stared you in the eye before you ate them. Laura played a good knife and fork. And a good glass, too. She was not the type to get her energy from low-calorie dishes. Her whole body had kept the vibrant hum of the Old World, which I verified when she slid into my comfortable bed. Making love with her was like experiencing John Coltrane's "Olé" live and in the flesh.

While we were dozing off in each other's arms, images projected themselves on my mental screen. The sign, red; the faces, Parker, Clementine, Exu, Nordvensen, Melody, Mona. I fell asleep and when I woke up I was alone. Laura's beeper must have beckoned her. It was six o'clock in the morning. I stumbled to the refrigerator, drank a Perrier with lemon, and called my black angel.

"Good morning, Mona."

"I was asleep but I had a feeling you were going to call me. What's happening? You okay?"

"Yes. Things are getting a little complicated. What's happening with you, babe?"

"No problem. Everything's cool. Do you know about Melody?"

"Yes . . ."

"Her drawings are terrifying . . ."

"I can imagine. Are you scared?"

"A little. I don't like this story. It's like going back to Africa, diving into time. I was just dreaming I had lost my head and it was hanging by the hair against a white wall, the blood running."

"Did it look like the mask at Bashma's?"

"Something like that, plus the blood . . . But listen, now I remember, there was a little cavity like the one in which you found the key for the locker. And somebody was putting something in my head, like in a radio . . ."

"A transistor?"

"Yeah, right . . . And my movements became mechanical, like a robot. It's time for you to take my head apart."

"I am on my way to Kingston but I'll come right back. Call me whenever you feel like it and don't worry. I'm onto something."

"Be careful, Zulu."

"You too, Mona. I lick your stomach."

"And your ankles . . ."

"And your neck . . ."

"And your eyes . . ."

"And your lips . . ."

"And your spine . . ."

"And your asshole . . ."

"And my cunt . . . Zulu. I am coming . . . Jump in the sky and come back to me like Dickman . . ."

I slept another two hours, got the report from the lab, and went back to Clementine's after gulping a cowboy's breakfast and drinking a quart of coffee.

I didn't forget the cigars nor the Jamaican rum. Better not cut corners when you are dealing with the spirit world. I found Clementine preparing lunch for her tigers. She was mixing the contents of a few cans with bread soaked in milk.

"Would you like some?"

"Meow, but no thank you. I prefer fruit."

Clementine plucked a mango from the fruit basket, got her wooden board and her knife. We took our offerings to Exu, then sat down in the armchairs. The sun still had not circumvented the building.

"So?"

"Neither the hair nor the nails belonged to her."

"That's what I thought, she bought somebody else's soul. A dead person, probably."

"I met a strange guy."

"There are plenty of them . . . Any dreams?"

"Everybody is dreaming, drawing."

"Magic activates strange things. We are full of unused images. When we come in contact with the magic world, they emerge."

"Sounds promising . . ."

"You've got to let the images go. If you hang on to them they will drag you down irreparably."

"I will try my best . . ."

"What is your next stop?"

"Jamaica."

"Bon voyage, son . . ."

I left Clementine feeling moved. This woman had an understanding of the invisible world, which seemed huge compared to the world I could see with my eyes. I started to hope that Exu would like the cigars. They were Partagases. I also hoped that he wouldn't get smashed on the rum, which had been recommended by the barman at Trader Wick's.

6

In the evening, after barely escaping three car accidents, I was quietly getting loaded with a rum cocktail beside the swimming pool of the Courtleigh Hotel, all white walls and green cascades. I had ordered a second glass for my host, Exu. I thought I might need his protection. I had a light dinner of grilled fish in the excellent restaurant of the hotel and went out into Kingston's pulsating reggae beat.

I hadn't asked for a car at the hotel. I wanted to choose a driver myself, someone I got a feel for, since Black River was all the way on the other side of the island. That was where the voodoo center was located, in the green mountains that Bashma and Kate had visited three times.

I was offered dope, women, and Swiss watches at ridiculously low prices, but this was no time to get high.

A beautiful Rastaman was taking a nap in the front seat of his Impala, his feet hanging out the window.

"Are you free for the night?"

"Two hundred and fifty dollars. My name is Ben."

"I'm Zulu. One hundred and fifty."

"I'll take you anywhere you want for a hundred and seventy-five."

I got in his car, in front; we hit hands before leaving the infernal-sound city. Ben made a quick stop to allow me to acquire some basics: a .38 and a sharp knife.

"How long will it take to get to Black River?"

"A little less than four hours."

Ben played a Peter Tosh cassette. His sound system wasn't too bad. He lit up a fragrant fat spliff. I took a few hits and kicked back, enjoying the black night split open by his headlights. I was thinking of Clementine, of her pleasant face with the air of a woman who had been around.

Two hours later we pulled up in front of a little greasy spoon at the edge of the jungle and ordered a glass of rum with a very spicy jerked pork. A hibiscus bush had taken over the cabin, which was half buried in the trees and vegetation. It looked like a truck stop. The drivers were getting drunk, naked down to the waist, watching a beautiful girl dancing alone in the night. A crackling speaker was spitting out a Bob Marley tune.

I always had the luck to run into people that fitted well within my investigations. When we got back in the car, I mentioned voodoo to Ben. He seemed to know a good deal about it. He said his grandmother had been a practitioner. She was retired now, but lived surrounded by a few disciples. She was very respected on the island. He told me a dozen impressive stories while maneuvering his car around the hairpin turns of a little mountain road. The perfume of the night was incredible. I sniffed it up with wide-open nostrils. A guy dressed all in white was standing arms akimbo in the middle of the road. Ben slammed on the brakes. The guy survived thanks only to Ben's quick reflexes.

There was a little group of people gathered around him, a woman lying in her own blood, two smashed cars. Ben pulled closer and we got out of the car and found ourselves with razor blades at our throats. The rest went very fast, and I woke up at dawn, lying in a ditch, face to face with a snake who slithered away in disdain. I had blood on my face, intense pain in the abdominal area, and the feeling that my ribs had been bashed with a tree trunk. With difficulty, I propped myself up on my elbows. The road was deserted. No taxi, no Ben. I ran my hand through my hair and stopped short. A crazy barber had shaved my temples, and when I discovered that the haircut had been followed by a manicure, I realized I had stumbled right into the magical universe. They hadn't even bothered to remove my weapons, as though mine were powerless against theirs. I still had my money, my credit cards, the key to my hotel room. But my suit was only good for the garbage.

I could hear water running nearby. I crawled toward it. Each movement hurt like hell. A spring cascaded on some pebbles. I washed my face in it, smoked a bit of a cigar, tried to get up but the abdominal pains were so bad I couldn't stand upright. I opened my shirt and discovered, on my stomach, probably traced with my own blood, the sign of the locket. I rubbed my stomach until it disappeared and rebuttoned my shirt. I heard a few cars pass by.

It took me a full hour to get up and make my way—with the gait of Frankenstein's monster—to the road. Nothing seemed broken, which was surprising.

A blue van carrying reeds pulled up. It was driven by a

young guy who looked and whistled like an Indian blackbird. The charming *avis* helped me get in and gave me something to drink. I told him I'd had an accident and that my car had been stolen. It sounded perfectly normal to him. Some parts of the island are still run by pirate law and Her Majesty's Navy had stopped cruising this area a long time ago.

The ride ended up in Mandeville, where I was able to buy some fresh clothes. Since they had already gotten hold of my soul in the form of my hair and nails, I figured I had nothing to lose by pursuing my trip till the end.

I found another driver, who dropped me off, an hour and a half later, in front of a group of houses scattered on the mountain. The poor fellow was shaking at the wheel, so dense was the population of gods in that part of the jungle.

A man with transparent skin came up to me. I asked for Clesh, he told me to follow him, invited me inside one of the houses, and disappeared. I made sure my blaster was in good shape, that it was still loaded and that, if need be, civilization could manifest itself in its less magical incarnations. I had the feeling I was suffering from a tropical fever. I was sweating and shaking, but that wasn't going to stop me from shooting a wor- shiper of Satan between the eyes.

I heard whispering. A head appeared by the half-open door. The abdominal pain was so strong that I wondered if I had been poisoned, but they could easily have finished me off with a bat, a razor blade, or a bullet in the neck, so why bother removing a piece of my soul?

An older woman, very skinny, walked in, watching me, leaning on the shoulder of a girl. She seemed to have suffered a lot; her hands were twisted by arthritis; still, she gave the feeling of undeniable strength.

"What do you want?" she asked without hostility.

"Ben, a cabdriver, gave me this address. I believe that a spell has been cast on me. I feel ill and I need help."

She saw the lock missing in my hair, looked at my fingernails.

"Are you in pain already?"

"Yes, my stomach. Really bad."

"Do you wish an encounter with the Father of the Gods?"

"The sooner the better."

"When did they cut your nails and hair?"

"Last night."

"Undoing a spell is very expensive."

"I know. I have the money."

"A thousand dollars . . ."

"Do you want it now?"

"No . . . after the work is done . . . I am going to see if the Father of the Gods is ready to receive you. He is a powerful hungan."

"I know."

She vanished. Without speaking, the young woman was staring at me with her huge black eyes. I was eager to see this man face-to-face, to see if he was indeed the Father of the Gods or the Father of the Devils. Unless he was burning the candles at both ends. I looked around for a sign similar to that of the locket.

The older woman came back to get me. She told me to follow her into a round house replete with central pole, an altar with offerings, images of gods, stylized snakes painted on a white wall, African drums, bottles holding various liquids, oil lamps, candles. A man in his sixties, dressed in a dirty old pair of pants and a red shirt, was sitting on a wobbly rattan chair. The girl, who had come with us, pulled up a stool with a cushion on it for me and I sat down in front of the hungan. He watched with eyes that looked tired from fighting against evil forces.

His jaw, shaded by a week-old beard, was rhythmically shaking. His hands, resting on a black stick, were also shaky. It took me a few minutes to adjust to the darkness and his gaze upon me. To my surprise, his eyes were devoid of hate. His bright but dilated pupils formed two intense points of light in the darkness. This man didn't seem evil. I couldn't imagine him taking lives for power or money. His eyes had seen a lot of pain, yet he had a stable and deep gaze. They revealed the soul of his body, almost diluted in space.

"How did you get here?"

"A cabdriver sent me . . . Ben . . ."

I could tell the old man didn't believe a word of it.

"What do you have in your pocket?"

"Pictures."

"Show them to me."

I showed him the Polaroids. He examined them carefully, without any surprise, then gave them back to me.

"I wasn't able to save them," he explained. "The enemy is too powerful. He is a big hungan. His powers are awesome, his *envois-morts* cannot be sent back. Bashma and her friend came here three times. They stayed more than a week. I did everything I could to repel the evil forces, but I failed and now my body is failing too and pays the price of this terrible defeat."

"Why did you accept risking your life?"

"Because I am old and the spirits have always served me well. I repelled more bad spells than any other voodoo priest. I saved all those who came to me, except Bashma and Kate . . . I've never encountered such evil power . . . Never . . ."

"Have you ever heard of a hungan capable of killing a victim by stabbing a knife in his image reflected in a bowl?"

"Papa Mosso, from Port-au-Prince, used to do it. But he died thirty years ago. He was a terrifying sorcerer. Nobody dared confront him. Baron-Samedi himself seemed to obey him."

"Baron-Samedi?"

"The Warden of the Dead, the Spirit of the Graves, the god that can only be invoked outside the *humfo,* the temple, because its manifestations are terrifying. He can be found at midnight, at the crossroads, in the countryside."

"Who succeeded Papa Mosso?"

"All the hungans he worked with are dead. None of them had his power."

"How did he die?"

"They say that one night, during a ritual on the graves, Baron-Samedi became jealous of Papa Mosso's powers and that the ground opened and swallowed him."

My palms and spine were dripping with sweat. I had no desire to smile like a vain student.

"How do you know these things?"

"I repelled death spells sent by disciples of Papa Mosso. I am known throughout the Caribbean for my white power. People come to see me from everywhere, including from Europe."

"You live modestly . . ."

"I live with the spirits. I only have to support my *humfo.*"

"Do you know what brought Bashma and Kate here?"

"The good hungans know me . . . In Miami . . . in New York . . ."

I remained silent, looking at the temple, the centerpost, axis of this strange world, magic elevator between the heavens and hell, and I understood the Father of the Gods must have traveled back and forth more than once. A cricket was chirping, its song amplified by the silence.

"I was attacked on my way here. My body is in pain."

"It's nothing. A *trempé* with a few words will reverse the spell."

"A *trempé?*"

"Macerated plants."

"Has a death spell been sent against me?"

"No, but it may happen at any time . . . Are you a relative of Bashma's?"

"A friend."

"Aren't you afraid to die searching for the truth?"

"Yes, but I can't help it. I am a good sorcerer myself in my own line of work and I don't give up easily."

"One of the reasons why I failed against the forces of evil is that I could only act by defending Bashma and Kate. If I had been able to counterattack directly, engage in a magic fight with the author of this death spell, I might have succeeded. That's why evil forces are so powerful. The one that triggers them is always safe. But when the magic fight takes place, one of the parties has to die."

"I understand. If I were able to identify the origin, would you be willing to . . ."

"Yes, I would do it, even if I were to end up burning in hell. There are terrifying forces that I have never used, although I know them, having fought them all my life."

The Father of the Gods straightened, jumped up, and ran three times around the centerpost, hollering an extraordinarily powerful cry. He asked me to undress. With the tip of his stick he traced a circle around me, pronouncing phrases I didn't understand. My body started to shake increasingly more violently, sweat was pouring out of each pore of my skin, my teeth were chattering, my eyes rolled back in my head, and I fell on the cool ground. I completely abandoned myself to the tremors, but remained conscious.

The Father of the Gods lit a fire and boiled some water in a clay pot. He took a handful of leaves from a basket covered with a chipped plate and threw them in the water muttering an unintelligible formula. He touched my body in various places. The shaking progressively abated, and when the potion was ready he washed my entire body with it, from the head down. I completely lost track of time and fell into a deep sleep.

I woke up just before dawn. I was wrapped in a rough blanket. An oil lamp was burning near me and the young woman I had seen the day before was looking at me with her dark and intense eyes. She soon disappeared and came back carrying a bowl containing a bitter beverage.

"Drink."

She gave me three bananas. I ate them and got dressed. She was watching me without curiosity. I had the feeling that she was only making sure my movements were well coordinated.

The old woman came in. I pulled out a wad of bills. She shook her head no.

"The Father of the Gods took you under his protection. You are his son. Come back as soon as you are in possession of the information he needs."

I kissed the two women and realized how light I felt. The pain had disappeared.

My driver was waiting for me, asleep on the backseat. The girl brought him a bowl of coffee and a piece of cake. Just as we were about to leave she came up to the car window and told me:

"My name is Polynice."

"Mine is Zulu."

"Come back soon, Zulu. The Father of the Gods must not leave us. He is a very good man."

She stroked my hand and her smile vanished. We drove down to the valley. The jungle came to life in an immense rustling.

I missed my plane but found a seat on the next flight. I had never felt so vibrant, so alert.

My faithful lieutenants were waiting for me. We drove through the airport, sound system blasting. *Serious Tits* was obviously not to everybody's taste. I still hadn't learned the art of discretion.

To be back on the interstate, in familiar territory, was the strangest return I had yet experienced.

"You look like you spent your time sucking on cocktails by a swimming pool," Lita said.

"Right," agreed the crazy rapper.

"You even had the time to get a real hip-hop haircut while you were away."

"Take me to the morgue, I've got to check on something. Then we'll go to the Palace for a serious lunch."

I called Mona. She was still asleep.

"Hi, jasmine flower."

"Are you coming to get some of my honey?"

"Meet us at the Palace. We'll have a feast."

"Okay. Give me an hour."

"Everything okay?"

"I am scared."

"Everything will be fine."

"I hope so."

There's nothing like walking down the cold corridors of the morgue to make you appreciate being alive. Gordon, the attendant, seemed to have already passed on to the other side. He was a big chalky fellow who seemed overly protective of his customers. Still, he couldn't refuse to open the drawers for me. He knew that Brad and Joe were behind me.

I started with Bashma. I immediately saw that the nails of her bluish hands had been cut as well as a lock of hair near the neck, small details that I had failed to notice when I had first examined her. Same thing for Kate. The Death Expediter had zealous assistants who took care of the menial chores. It occurred to me that the curious who had been watching the bogus accident back in Jamaica and who had been in charge of trimming my nails and hair were not much older than the Miami spray-painter. So there was a whole youthful infrastructure supporting the Death Expediter in his terrible mission.

"When it's your turn to lie in a drawer," Gordon said nicely, "I'll make sure nobody bothers you."

"Too kind of you, Gordon. You are a really responsible guy."

"You're right. I am very reliable," he said, holding the front door wide open for me.

Miami air never smelled so good. But I felt Gloria was a bit cool to me. I had overextended my three days' credit.

"I need an extra couple of days."

"You're always welcome to try your luck."

That was reassuring and I promised myself I would try it as soon as the Death Expediter would give me a break. We sat down on the terrace and ordered all around. Roy had chicken salad, Lita and I the grilled Maui tuna, served on a bed of spinach, and a bottle of Chablis. This called for a good cigar, and just then I saw Petra appear out of the blue. She offered me a box of three cigars tied with a yellow ribbon.

"You must have a direct line to Castro; it's impossible to find twisted cigars nowadays."

"Did I ever mention to you he was crazy in love with me when I was young?"

"No, but I believe it."

I slipped a roll of dollars into her palm. She saluted me with a curtsy and went on her way.

A cab pulled up. Mona stepped out. Something was wrong. She was ashen, which in people of our color takes the hue of aluminum. I jumped. She threw herself in my arms and burst into tears. Stroking her hair, I felt a missing patch of hair on her neck and I immediately saw that some of her fingernails had been cut short.

"They came during the night. I didn't feel anything . . . They are going to kill me . . . Like Bashma . . . They are going to kill me . . ."

"They are not going to kill anybody. I am onto them."

Mona lifted her eyes and saw that some of my own hair was missing too.

"You too . . . Why? Why did they kill Bashma, Kate, and now . . . ?"

"I learned a lot of things these last few days . . . I am not alone anymore . . ."

I pulled a chair next to me and kept Mona in my arms. She slowly calmed down. I told her about my trip.

Mona nibbled from my plate and drank a little wine.

"And the kid who spray-painted the walls?" I asked.

"The motherfucker has disappeared. I watched for any new signs. Nothing since you left. You must have scared him off."

I telephoned Mono to find out if the stolen master tapes had been found.

"Any news about the tapes?"

"Nada. The distribution company is putting pressure. They are prepared to launch a mega ad campaign, the editors of all the glossies are on my back, and I am screwing up the best deal of my life because of some little motherfucker. Okay . . . I gotta go . . . All the lines are ringing . . . Later, Zulu."

He hung up before I had time to ask him to put on

Pedro, the sound engineer. I called back. The new secretary had a charming voice.

"Yeah. Pedro speaking."

"Listen, man, were there any cuts for *Pure Steel* that haven't been used on the album?"

"Yeah. Two . . . But even if you remix them, you'll never make anything out of them . . ."

"Can you make a copy of them for me? I'll pick it up right now."

"I'm telling you, you're going to be disappointed."

I took Mona and Live Crew along and when we pulled in at Rapadise Records, Pedro had just finished copying the songs. I thanked him for his trouble and took the cassette.

I slipped it into the tape player. It definitely wasn't as good as the rest. But all of a sudden the lyrics of the second cut hit me:

> *Kate! Kate! Kate!*
> *Tell me! Tell me! Tell me!*
> *Why? Why? Why?*
> *Your daddy hated red . . .*
> *Kate! Kate! Kate!*
> *Tell me! Tell me! Tell me!*
> *Why? Why? Why?*
> *Your daddy liked blood . . .*
> *Kate! Kate! Kate!*
> *Tell me! Tell me! Tell me!*
> *Why? Why? Why?*
> *Joe hated magic . . .*
> *Kate! Kate! Kate!*
> *Tell me! Tell me! Tell me!*
> *Why? Why? Why?*
> *Joe dug no witches . . .*

I slowed the car down to forty, until everything connected and the old internal hard disk spat out the following
information:

Red-Communists / Joe-McCarthy / Kate-Kate

"Do you think it has something to do with magic?" Lita
asked.

I smiled, called Brad, and asked him to get rid of whoever was in his office right now.

I drove down Collins Avenue full speed and parked in
the police parking lot. I took the cassette and the boom box with
me and stormed into Brad's office like an antiterrorist squad
boarding a plane.

"Lower the fucking volume!" screamed Brad.

I rewound it and finally got to the right lyrics.

"Fucking interesting."

Two minutes later we were poring over the computer's
files, calling up the complete and unexpurgated biography of
James Henning, Kate's father.

Very active during the McCarthy witch-hunt, he had
been suspended because of an "incident" that had occurred
during the investigation of an actor suspected of procommunist
sympathies.

"A small slip occurred," Brad murmured, "leading to the
thespian's unfortunate demise."

"So it goes. Happened November 2, 1954."

"Just a month before McCarthy was condemned by the
Senate."

"The victim was one Erwin Zab, age twenty-three."

The most interesting detail was that Mr. Zab had practiced voodoo and that various objects of cultism had been found
in his residence, as well as certain accoutrements typically used
in black magic.

Henning claimed in his defense that he had lost control

after discovering these objects. Even more curious: Henning died in 1962 following a long disease his doctors were never able to identify.

"Similar death to Kate, similar death to Bashma. Could it have been Kate they were after, and not Bashma?"

"Revenge."

"Whose revenge? You think it had something to do with someone who had been practicing voodoo with Erwin Zab?"

Brad hit more keys and came up with another interesting fact: Kate's mother died two years later, under similar circumstances, and Kate, then three years old, had been raised under an assumed name in a boarding school. Four months ago she had made an official request to regain her legal name, as she was entitled to by law, and that's when the Death Expediter caught up with her.

"The question is, how did this revenger find out about Bashma's song?"

"Maybe by accident," Brad said.

"I don't believe in that kind of accident . . . Did Zab have a family?"

"He had a sister. Do you want us to locate her for you?"

"The sooner the better."

"What about your trip?"

I filled him in on the highlights.

"Crazy story."

"Feel free to call me anytime."

I went out more discreetly than I had come in. Now it became clear to me, as I was walking toward my car, why Bashma's apartment had been cleaned out. Kate must have given her all the documents concerning her father for safekeeping, and the Death Expediter didn't want to miss a thing. If he was the one who stole the master tapes of *Pure Steel,* he must have been disappointed. On the other hand, there was a chance he would send someone to inspect the warehouse of Rapadise Records. I asked Brad to have his cops put it under surveillance.

"It looks like we're beginning to have a handle on the case," Lita said.

"We're making progress."

"This thing is whack," Roy said.

Mona, impressed by the events, remained silent.

"I have to take a break," I said. "I need to buy myself a new suit."

"We didn't want to tell you, but when you got off the plane, Lita and I, we thought you were looking real cheap," Roy said.

7

To confront the forces of evil, French boxing might seem a bit lightweight, but I needed to get back into shape, so I spent three hours at Roger's, punching ghosts. Lita was making progress. Brad and Joe were threatening to become as good as I was.

"A bit tight today," Roger observed.

"I know . . ."

"Zulu, you have to defend my reputation. If any Tom, Dick, or Harry beats you up, I'll have to pack my bags and go back to Paris."

"I'll come more often."

"Tough case?"

"Rather, yes. My opponent is an expert in a martial art that kills without visible fight."

"I told you drugs don't mix with training. You got high in Kingston."

"I mean seriously."

Roger's answer was to land a hook to my throat that I had trouble blocking. Monsieur Camembert had a pretty straightforward sense of dialectic. He let me draw my own conclusions from this flurry and turned his interest to Lita and Roy.

When we were done we all went out to drink a guayaba juice at a Cuban fruit stand.

"This story is beginning to make waves. The DA consulted with a bishop," Joe said.

"You're kidding," Brad said.

"No, apparently the church has special weapons against Satan."

Joe had a vicious smile. His pale face of debauched and ambitious materialism clearly showed that as soon as he had replaced the DA, his own methods would be more efficient.

"So, what's the story with Erwin Zab's sister?" I asked.

"We'll locate her before the end of the day," Brad said.

"Am I soon going to have something concrete to put under the DA's nose?" Joe asked.

"Everything is in Zulu's hands. My men are in over their heads."

"Let the DA fool around with his bishop while we are working."

We each went our separate ways. I gave Live Crew a few hours' break and looked for a quiet place. Jill invited me over for tea. She had just finished a chocolate cake that would be out of the oven by the time I got there.

There was a hammock in the library, a calm and cool room overlooking the beautiful garden. I climbed into the hammock to sway and think. Live Crew had promised to join me later at Mona's.

Tea, English porcelain, books that somebody had actually read, silence. The flavor of chocolate was floating inside of me. I was gathering the threads. Erwin Zab's sister was the most important source of information. She must have known with whom her brother was practicing black magic and I was extremely interested in that person.

There was another lead, more uncertain, more complicated, that might get me nowhere: finding someone from Papa Mosso's entourage. But going to Port-au-Prince would be like searching for a grain of blue sand in the Gobi Desert.

Maybe Clementine could help me. I let my arm hang, fingers brushing the ground, and lifted my cellular phone to my ear.

"Clementine, it's Zulu."

"My son, what's happening?"

"Everything's been great. I almost got killed but a good *trempé* saved me."

"You are beginning to enter our world."

"Tell me, that voodoo priest you used to know in Port-au-Prince, was his name Papa Mosso, by any chance?"

"Papa Mosso . . . Yes . . . Papa Mosso, that was his name. How did you find out?"

"Since I've had a patch of hair excised from my skull and my fingernails pared, I am finding out a lot of things."

"Don't joke about that, son."

"Oh, right, sorry."

"You're in serious danger."

"I know, that's why I've got to move fast. Do you have any connections in Port-au-Prince?"

"I know a few people."

"I need to know as much as possible about Papa Mosso,

his disciples, his family, anybody who, one way or another, could lead me to him."

"I'll make some phone calls."

"Would you like to go to Haiti?"

"I don't go out much anymore."

"In one hour, a friend of mine will come and pick you up. She will drive you to the airport, will take care of your ticket, and will give you enough money to stay there as long as you need."

"It's nice of you, son, I'd love to go back to my country, but I am not sure to find what you're looking for."

"It doesn't matter, Clementine. In that case, it will be a present from me."

"I will be ready in an hour."

"Write down my phone number and call me anytime, for any reason. Maybe you can save my skin, Clementine . . ."

"I know, son. That's why I am going."

I emptied my teapot and told myself that the best way to wait, since everything was in the hands of my pals for the time being, was to call Gloria.

"No mail, Zulu."

"Come and meet me at Jill's."

"I'm in the middle of my shift."

I gave her the address, trusting her talents of improvisation. I went to the kitchen to see Jill, who was devouring a huge novel by Fernando del Paso while stirring a mixture of salmon and herbs with one hand.

"What are you making?"

"A salmon terrine with soaked bread. It's a southern dish."

"Your chocolate cake was aces. Do you have a dinner tonight?"

"Yes, friends of mine."

"Can I borrow a bedroom?"

"I'd have to have it soundproofed."

"We'll be quiet as mice."

"Take the big studio on the third floor."

"Right on."

A bit of sauce spattered on the book.

"You should try baking your books in the oven, with all the stuff you spill on them."

"I've thought about it."

I gave her a kiss on her double chin and went upstairs. There was no one better than Jill. The studio was all wood paneled, the floor covered with colorful Mexican rugs and a supercomfortable low-slung, king-sized bed. I called my beautiful limousine driver.

"So, gorgeous, you split right after getting laid."

"I had an important customer who was waiting for me in Atlantic City. A guy you can't refuse a ride."

"I see. What about me, would you refuse me a ride?"

"No."

"I had a great night."

"Me too. You are getting better."

"Thanks . . . You are going to go pick up a woman called Clementine. I want you to give her five thousand dollars, and make a reservation for her on the first flight to Port-au-Prince."

"I don't have that much in my bank account."

"I'm wiring you the money posthaste. Put her on the plane and pick her up on the way back."

I took her account number, gave her the address, took a shower, and slipped between the sheets that smelled of fresh lavender. By this time, the Death Expediter had certainly received the materials he needed to add Mona and me to his list of victims, and that notion didn't exactly thrill me. To put the brakes on my fate, I took a mininap.

It felt like a cool, then a warm, breeze, here and there on my skin. It seemed as if angels were running their soft down all over my body. Lips stroked me, a mouth explored me, and a burning body glided across mine. My tongue was navigating in a sweet-tasting mouth, and my salivary glands came at the same time as those of Gloria, whom I recognized when I opened my eyes.

The perfume of her body intoxicated me. I turned over and went in search of the sources of the perfume. A few light kisses made the attar flow more strongly. That girl was a real distillery of intense and wild fragrances. I became drunk on her with all my senses. Our music began to make its way down the wood partitions. Gloria's nails drew Chinese characters on my skin. Our heat intermingled, promising frenetic messages. My whole face disappeared between her thighs. My tongue, fingers, nose, forehead improvised moves, slides, drifts that Gloria's screams pulled back to her epicenter. I stroked her stomach, thighs, breasts, neck, face, rump, back. She twisted her body like a dancer in trance and I let myself go to the pulse of my soul, losing myself to the cosmos.

The night came, Jill's friends left, and around four A.M., after our bodies had become acquainted with each Mexican rug, after we had outgrown the bed, we finally reached the seventh sky in an ultimate orgasm.

A flood fell upon Miami, bringing all the smells of the earth up to our refuge. Gloria's eyes were open, deep, her mouth half agape; she was laughing, shaking with spasms tumbling like waves on the surface of a still water after a stone has been tossed in it.

About an hour later, I went to meet my jasmine flower at the Fruit Market. I felt fresh and in top shape. I slipped the rose in her hair, paid my respects to Speed, the good pimp, and we headed for Mona's little white house. She filled two glasses with

ice cubes and we sat down on the beat-up couch, on the deck.
The air was hot and humid, the local kids asleep. Only the old
insomniac was still watching his TV, taking in the breeze blowing on his deck. I loved that time when everything mellows out
for a few hours.

"Had a good day?"

"I am making progress. I discovered that Bashma was
killed by accident. She was keeping compromising documents at
her place."

"What about us? Why are they after us?"

"Because Bashma taped a rap that tells the whole story
but that is not on the master tape. Pedro and Mono removed two
songs and one of those is what they were after."

"So they stole the tapes for nothing?"

"They can always get money for them."

"I am scared. All night long I was scared. I am on the
lookout for every quiver of my body, the slightest change, as if
I was expecting to get ill any minute."

"The more you think about it, the easier you make it for
them. You are making yourself vulnerable to them."

"I can't help it."

I took her in my arms. She turned and cuddled against
me. It was the first time I had felt her so young, so fragile. I could
read fear in her eyes. She was tender and warm. I caressed her.
She moaned softly.

"As soon as I am with you, my anxiety leaves. I feel
good."

"Did you spend some of your money?"

She laughed.

"I can't get used to the idea it's all mine. This afternoon
I went shopping. I bought an emerald green leather miniskirt
and matching Italian pumps and I went to get a facial in Coral

Gables, where the rich chicks go. It was great. It was the first time I had that done. I felt like a queen. I fell asleep it was so good."

"You are going to be able to take it easy soon. Do you have any idea how much Speed would ask to let you go?"

"With your friends, you could scare him off and he would leave me alone."

"It's more simple and less risky to pay. Pimps like nothing better than to set an example."

"I heard it was around twenty thousand dollars."

"I talked to one of my lawyer friends. He can straighten things out with the IRS, but you'll still have to give them a good chunk of dough."

"I don't care, as long as I have some money ahead of me, for myself and to take care of Melody."

"Do you have any idea what you'd like to do?"

"I'd like to stay alive long enough to enjoy the dough. Otherwise, I can always have a marble headstone erected, like an Egyptian queen or a goddess."

It was my turn to laugh. The bourbon went down little by little. Our bodies calmed down, melted into the night. Mona opened my shirt, licked me around the belly button.

"I want you to fuck me," she said.

She undressed me completely. I slipped her miniskirt down, removed her T-shirt while I was kissing her chest and belly with my half-opened lips. She opened her legs, leaned against one of the couch's armrests. I licked her face and her eyes. She turned over. My tongue ran down the muscles of her neck up to the line of her short and thick hair. She moaned and slipped to the ground, supporting herself with her hands. My tongue followed the muscles along her spine, wandered around the small of her back, slipped between her buttocks to the delicately curled anus and her open cunt, at the edge of which pearled a few drops of desire. I licked her for a long time, tenderly. Her breathing came faster, her moans became louder.

"Take me in the ass," she whispered.

The cops are usually slow, but they often reach their goal. They also have the uncanny ability to get you at the wrong time, which is exactly what Brad did, calling me at ten past nine in the morning, while my limbs and soul were completely at one with those of Mona. I don't know how we had made it to the bed, but that's where I answered the call, while the gray cat was purring like the engine of a 747.

"At this time, who else but a cop—"

"Bingo!" Brad said.

"Better be worth it."

"Judge for yourself. Rachel Zab, 2376 Westwood Lane, Atlanta. She is an architect and works at home. Usually works until eight P.M. Divorced. One child, Aaron, twelve years old."

"Thanks, copper. I am jumping on the next plane. Ciao."

Mona didn't even wake up. Somebody could have come and straightened her hair in her sleep, she wouldn't even have stirred. What I did to her was a lot more gentle. She came in her sleep. I got dressed and woke up Live Crew to tell them they could sleep until I came back later in the evening. If they needed the car they could get it at the airport. I would leave the parking ticket under the seat, as usual.

I got dressed, left a message for Mona. I stuck a Post-it on her belly with these words:

"Your ass is as soft as paradise. It gave me wings and although I am not an angel myself, I will be back here around five A.M. Zulu."

I stopped by at Beach Pressing on the way, donned a

raspberry linen suit, a pistachio shirt, a night blue tie, and Rossetti pumps in woven leather of the same color. I left my artillery behind, reserved a seat on the next flight, and headed for Atlanta.

This charming city's airport was a regular nightmare, but what wouldn't I do in order to survive? I called Rachel Zab from the airport, told her I was an advertising executive who had just made his first million and that I was thinking of building a villa on the beach in Pensacola, to replace a wood cabin that belonged to my folks. They did actually own a stretch of sand and had retired in this spot favored by navy folks. With this half-lie, I promised myself I would visit them as soon as death stopped tailing me.

I took a cab and showed up at Rachel's. She was expecting me. She looked like she did all right for herself. One floor for her offices, three floors for her residence, her house was a big black cube, rather beautiful, in the middle of a garden kept immaculate by Chicano lawnmowers.

Rachel Zab was a young fifty. She received me in a large, almost empty room with pearl gray walls and carpet. A large canvas by Joan Mitchell glowed. The decor was minimalist: a metal and glass coffee table, a few art deco armchairs in anthracite leather, and an architect's portfolio on the table completed the decor. Rachel Zab was tall, well built, her Italian suit was of perfect cut; she had the face of a workaholic. Her mouth was very thin; her glasses by Giancarlo Ferre framed her bright eyes and rested on an imposing broken nose that was full of character. In short, that face and that body spelled one word: efficiency.

With a smile, she invited me to sit down. A young woman, also very elegant, came in and offered me a drink: fruit juice, pure malt, port, Perrier, champagne, or Bordeaux. I opted for Perrier/orange, my hostess took a carrot juice.

"Who recommended you to me?"

"My eyes."

"Quite a compliment."

The young woman poured my drink and asked me if I wanted to have a look at the portfolio, which she delicately placed on my lap. I leafed through it, taking my time. All the work was top-notch, very classy.

"Beautiful."

Rachel smiled at me.

"How big is your land?"

"Two and a half acres of sand, at Pensacola."

"Do you have any idea of the kind of house you would like?"

"One room, warehouse style. Everything open, everything visible."

"Original."

It was my turn to smile.

"Are you interested in voodoo?"

Some blush, others become agitated. Rachel started to shake all over. She needed a full minute to pull herself together.

"Who are you?" she screamed in a high-pitch yell.

I pulled out my PI's card.

"I am investigating old classified documents that may or may not have a connection with present events, and your brother's file is among those documents."

Rachel got up, poured herself a double scotch, which she immediately drained. She walked around the room with her glass.

"My brother was murdered by a cop . . . A cop like you!"

"I know, but I am neither a cop, nor am I Henning. I have utmost sympathy for those who had the courage to be part of the Infinity Movement. So please, don't insult me."

She sat down, looked straight into my black eyes. What she saw in them probably reassured her.

"I'm sorry, you are stirring such cruel memories . . ."

"I understand . . ."

"Would you like to go up to my apartment? We'll be more comfortable."

Rachel called the secretary, asked her to hold her calls. We walked up to the second floor. Hundreds of art books, walls painted Klein blue, a big worktable, everything a bit messy, a super sound system with futuristic speakers that must have cost a bundle. The armchairs and the couch in pink leather struck a cheerful note. There were hundreds of CDs lining the shelves, newspapers and magazines everywhere, and a de Kooning on the wall.

"We love the same painters. Maybe we'll get along."

"Really?" she said, surprised.

She took out a big red file, opened it on her worktable.

"Photos of Erwin . . . From a Tennessee Williams play he was in . . ."

The kid had had a passionate face, very expressive. She showed me other photos. There were also packs of letters, press clippings.

"He would have become one of the greats. He had the presence of a Brando, a Newman."

"McCarthy destroyed a generation of geniuses; he sullied others by compromising them. One of the blackest periods of our history."

"What do you want to know?"

"Everything you can tell me."

"Ask me questions . . ."

I looked at the de Kooning before beginning.

"Did you know your brother practiced voodoo?"

"Yes . . . Like many artists, he was emotionally fragile. Some consult clairvoyants, astrologists. Others, like Erwin, turn to action or what they believe to be action. There was in him a desire for power that couldn't be satisfied in life. Like many psychopaths, he thought he could manipulate the world directly, act on it with magic. His desire for power could only be expressed through that channel."

"How did he get involved with voodoo?"

"Erwin was homosexual. He met a man, older than him, at the time when he acted in the Tennessee Williams play. That man was a voodoo grand master whose power was terrifying. He initiated Erwin. I don't think Erwin was ever successful at it."

"What makes you say that?"

"We were very close. I was young and I followed everything he was doing with admiration. He talked to me about his doubts, of his inconclusive experiences."

"And how did he react?"

"He pressed on, he believed that one day he would really be possessed by Africa's gods . . . All this was a bit childish."

"Did you ever meet his master?"

"Once, I ran into them."

"Were they lovers?"

"I believe so."

"Would you describe this man for me?"

"He was black, brilliant. I believe he was teaching at Columbia University."

"Do you know his name?"

"No, Erwin always referred to him as 'the Father of the Gods.' "

"What did he teach?"

"Anthropology, I think."

My blood started to boil. I couldn't believe she was talking about Parker. Had he sent me to Clementine simply to manipulate me?

"Did this man belong to the Infinity Movement?"

"Yes, he introduced Erwin to it. For Erwin it was a great moment. He was entering an extraordinary elite and at the same time he thought he was gaining supreme power. In retrospect it's a horrible story."

"Do you have any document, any photo relating to this man?"

"I have a photo in which they are together. It's a bad, underexposed photo. I don't know if it'll be of any use to you."

Rachel rummaged through the documents and pulled out a photo with dented edges. I immediately recognized Parker. There was no mistake. Brave Professor Parker, inconsolable widower.

"Do you think there was a deep connection between this man and Erwin?"

"Yes, I think it was a passionate love affair."

"May I keep this photo?"

"Yes. You can keep it. I don't like it."

"Thank you. You've been a great help. You will probably contribute to saving a number of lives, including mine."

"I don't understand . . ."

"I will explain when everything is over."

"All right . . . I respect your silence . . . Delighted to have been able to assist you . . ."

"I will give you my phone number; call me if anything else comes to mind. Even an insignificant detail."

I wrote my phone number on a sketch pad that was on the table and went back to my cab. I took the first plane to New York and caught a cab to Parker's. I had the driver drop me nearby. I wanted to get into his apartment, and in order to achieve that, I had to make him come out. I wrote a note and paid a kid five bucks to deliver it. I invited Parker for dinner in a chic restaurant in the Village, as far away as I could think of. I wrote that I had finished my investigation and that I had fascinating revelations to tell him. I was almost certain his curiosity would be piqued. I reserved a table and arranged for him to be told upon his arrival that I would be a half-hour late. I bought a suitcase on Broadway and filled it with heavy objects.

Ten minutes later, dear old Professor Parker came out of his building and quickly turned toward Broadway, where he hailed a cab.

The same doorman, definitely a slow reader, was still plodding through the Stephen King novel.

"Good evening."

"You're out of luck, Mr. Parker just left."

"I told him I was going to pick him up. The old man's losing his marbles . . . I shouldn't speak like that of my uncle, but sometimes it drives me nuts . . ."

"At his age, it's normal."

"Man, this suitcase weighs a ton. Look at this. It's full of first editions he asked me to pick up at Stanford."

"I'll keep them for you."

"There's more than a hundred thousand dollars' worth of books in there."

"Books?"

"Very rare volumes."

"I'm sorry . . . I would take them up to his place, but I am alone."

I looked exasperated.

"Okay, I'll go myself, then."

The doorman opened a drawer, rummaged through the keys, found the ones he was looking for. I went upstairs, dropped off the suitcase, removed the key to the apartment, replaced it with one of my mine that looked vaguely similar, and went back to give the doorman the keys back.

"Thanks, bud."

"You're welcome."

It started to rain. I hid across the street from the building, waiting for an opportunity to get back inside without drawing the attention of the doorman. A few minutes later a cab pulled up, and a woman came down into the lobby walking with canes. The doorman opened his umbrella and helped the woman to the cab. While he folded her legs and put away her canes, I slipped inside and ran up the stairs. On my way, I pictured a room filled with *pots-têtes,* plastic bags with my nail clippings and hair and those of Mona. A bowl, a ritual dagger, and all sorts of ignoble statuettes pierced with needles.

8

The two-bedroom apartment occupied the southern side of the building. I didn't notice anything out of the ordinary in the living room. Books, books, books. A few African artifacts. A shield, a spear, statuettes, a TV, a pair of ugly but comfortable armchairs, a couch, a recliner. The study was also full of books, from floor to ceiling. The desk was clean, except for a checkbook and some bills. Obviously, Parker didn't do a lot of work anymore. I opened the drawers of a Chinese bureau used to store letters and documents.

There was a pile of correspondence in a cardboard box. I read three letters. They were from his wife. All the letters seemed to be from her. I closed the last drawer and went on to the bedroom. The heavy curtains were drawn, keeping the room in darkness. I suddenly heard someone fooling around with the front door lock. It took a little longer than it would with a key but the intruder eventually broke into the apartment. I unscrewed the bulb from the ceiling fixture and hid behind the thick curtains.

The intruder quickly inspected the living room, the study, and finally came into the bedroom, tried the switch, cursed, took out a flashlight, looked around the room. I caught a glimpse of him from behind the curtain. Twenty years old, jeans, leather jacket, curly hair. He was not a thief but a delivery-man. He opened the walk-in closet, turned on the light, shoved in a cardboard box that he tried to hide behind a couple of suitcases. It would have been easy for me to put the collar on him, but I had a feeling I would learn more by letting him go. Which is what I did. He left, closing the front door behind him. I screwed the bulb back in and peeked into the cardboard box. In it was everything I had come looking for. *Pots-têtes,* photos of Kate, her father, Bashma, me, and Mona. There were a few impassioned letters signed "Erwin." A clay bowl, a ritual dagger, some candles, an image of Baron-Samedi.

I opened the *pots-têtes.* They contained hair and nail clippings, each set probably corresponding to one of the photos, which seemed to have been taken with a zoom. I recognized Kate's hair, Bashma's hair, the hair of a man who must have been Henning, and mine. One thing I noted was that there was a lot less hair of mine than had been cut from my head. Also, half the nail clippings were missing. But there was enough damaging evidence to mislead a stupid detective. Parker was being framed, and frankly, if I had come after the other visitor, instead of before, I would have had good reason to suspect the old man. But I had moved faster and I was beginning to see some light. I had probably been tailed the first time I had come here. The

Death Expediter had assumed I would find Rachel, who had only pretended to be terrified. She had probably tried to manipulate me on orders of the Death Expediter. I had to pretend to be sucked in. I closed the box, put it back where I had found it, and left the apartment while the doorman's back was turned. That doorman deserved to be fired. I walked a little to see if I wasn't being tailed, and grabbed a cab.

On my way to the Village, I decided to go back to East Hampton. So I called Laura to have her pick me up at the restaurant in an hour and a half. I also asked her for a .38.

Parker was delighted to see me. Calm and relaxed. We ordered stuffed crabs and a leg of lamb with a bottle of Saint-Emilion.

"Are you making any progress?"

"Yes . . . This may come as a surprise, but they're trying to frame you—"

"Me!"

"Yes. I have been sent after you with a picture of you and Erwin Zab."

"What a terrible story. He was a good actor and a nice boy. My wife and I liked him very much."

"Do you know which members of the Infinity Movement he was connected with?"

"He was our youngest member. As I said, everybody liked him. He was full of life, very funny."

"Did you know he was homosexual?"

"Yes . . ."

"Did he have a relationship with any of the group members?"

"I have no idea."

"Did you have enemies in the movement?"

"Not that I know of. We shared a common ideal and

professionally I was the only anthropologist, so there was no competition on that ground."

"What do you know about Nordvensen?"

"He was brilliant, a first-class scientist. His career was destroyed by McCarthy. He never recovered. Even after the Senate's decision, he didn't come back. Luckily for him, he had money."

"Do you remember speaking about voodoo with him or with Erwin?"

"No . . . I don't think so . . ."

"They knew that was your field, though."

"Of course, but I don't remember any curiosity about it from either of them. Nordvensen was a major scientist and for people like that voodoo is merely considered superstition."

I took out the photo Rachel had given me and showed it to Parker. He held it in his hands, stared at it for a long time without a word, then looked at me with emotion.

"Where did you find it?"

"It was the first link in a chain that was to point to you as the Death Expediter. The police might have fallen for it."

"In other words, I am lucky that it was you."

"I couldn't understand why you would have sent me to Clementine."

"But for a while you believed it . . ."

"Enough to go visit your apartment. The dinner was a pretense."

"I won't hold it against you."

"When you know that your life and the lives of your loved ones are in danger, you tend to act impulsively."

"Would this photo have been enough to implicate me?"

"No, but the box that was brought to your home about an hour ago would have . . ."

"What are you talking about?"

"While I was there, a 'deliveryman' came to hide *pots-têtes,* a clay bowl, a ritual dagger, photos of past and future victims, and various accessories in your closet."

"Are they still there?"

"Yes . . . Would you agree to play the game till the end?"

"What would that involve?"

"I am going to organize your bogus arrest. Our opponents will relax their watch and I will have more room to maneuver. You will be under the protection of the police."

Parker hesitated for a few moments.

"Something escapes me . . ."

"What is it?"

"Suppose you are able to identify this Death Expediter. How will you act against him? I can't imagine this country's justice system indicting on the basis of magic weaponry . . . The courts would laugh in your face. The nation's solid rationalism would play against you, against the victims, and in spite of all the deaths, the case would undoubtedly be dismissed."

"You are absolutely right and before we knew it, my friends and I would undoubtedly join the ranks of the victims."

"Right . . . So . . ."

"My intention is to fight them with their own weapons."

"Impossible!"

I paused to sample the leg of lamb and honor the Saint-Emilion Château Cheval Blanc 1961, which was going to cost me a small fortune. Parker did the same, watching me with veiled eyes.

"Clementine used to know a very powerful sorcerer . . . Papa Mosso . . ."

"The name sounds vaguely familiar . . . It was a long time ago . . . in Haiti . . ."

"Right . . . Clementine is there right now . . . She is on his trail . . . He died about thirty years ago but there must be someone . . . family . . . or a disciple . . . and my guess is that person is the Death Expediter."

"Let's hope Clementine will find something . . . She is a pure and good woman . . . intelligent . . . She knows a lot of people . . . She will succeed."

"Time is crucial."

"I will help you."

"All right. I'll pretend I'm going back to your place. You have dessert, maybe a little cognac, and then go home. Later in the afternoon the police will come to arrest you. It may seem a little obvious."

"Never mind . . . You are brave . . . Reckless perhaps, but I wouldn't want anything to happen to you . . ."

"Me neither."

"Are you frightened?"

"Yes."

Parker smiled. I called the maître d', gave him my credit card.

"I am on my way, Parker. See you later."

"You are sly . . ."

I called Live Crew. There was a message from Clementine. She was onto something, but nothing definite yet.

Laura, beautiful as ever, was waiting for me behind the wheel of her limo.

"Back already? Are you free for the night?"

I kissed her.

"Did you get the piece?"

"Of course. I told you I have connections."

"If you don't want to have sex with a dead man, get a move on."

"Where are we going?"

"East Hampton."

"Same place?"

"Yup."

"Any problems?"

"Only serious ones."

"I thought so, you look tense."

"I am fighting against Baron-Samedi."

"Never heard of him."

"Never mind, I'll tell you all about him between the sheets."

"I love to fuck with you."

"Then next time try to stay until breakfast."

"I promise."

Night was falling. We drove out of the city. I watched Laura's profile against a background of cloudy dusk and thought she might be the last beautiful woman I would ever see.

There was weather on Long Island. I asked Laura to stop about a mile away from Nordvensen's house. I checked the gun and headed out, hidden by the night and the dunes. The wind was moaning gloomily. In the distance, the Death Expediter's villa, all lit up, was isolated like a temple. Parker was right, I couldn't imagine the judiciary struggling with this case. It would be impossible to prove the cause of the deaths or even the means used by the criminal. Nor could I imagine the Death Expediter standing in front of a jury with his clay bowl and his dagger.

By the time I got to the house, the howling of the wind was overwhelming. Maybe Baron-Samedi had come in person in honor of my death sentence and Mona's.

I climbed the stairs. The house seemed empty. Nordvensen was not swinging in his hammock. I could see a huge kitchen, a bedroom, a bathroom all in marble with a Jacuzzi, an office. A staircase led down to the basement, where there might be a garage, maybe for a boat.

I walked back along the house, light as a cat. I pushed the handle of the glass door; it slid smoothly. I went in, closed the door behind me, listened. Silence. A slight odor of red peppers and fish made me think that Nordvensen had just finished dinner. My Polaroid had been removed from the wall. It had been replaced by a clay sculpture of a young and beautiful face, Erwin Zab.

A dishwasher was running in the kitchen, practically noiselessly. I turned it off for a second, opened it. There were only two pieces of silverware, one plate, one glass, and a small custard cup. Nordvensen was alone. He must be in the basement.

I went into the office and took the staircase down, pausing on each step. I heard whispers. I came closer. It was Nordvensen's voice. We were separated by a door. Nordvensen spoke fast, but I thought I recognized some words in French; he seemed to be saying magic formulas in Creole. His voice quivered slightly. I pushed the door handle down, opened the door a crack. I could see Nordvensen's profile. He was dressed in a long red tunic. The room was round, with a wooden pillar in the center. The candles were illuminating images of gods and, as on other voodoo altars I had seen, there were various offerings. On a long wooden table were wax statuettes pierced with long needles.

Nordvensen was standing above a clay bowl balanced on a pillar. I couldn't see any image on the surface of the water but the incantations were probably aimed at bringing forth a face. Mona's or mine. Nordvensen was so concentrated that he didn't see me come in. I moon-walked around him, standing off at an angle so that I could watch the surface of the liquid. I was hypnotized by that bowl. Gun in hand, ready to shoot, I waited.

Nordvensen was shaking. I could see droplets of sweat on his temples and on his neck. He kept reciting the same long chant, over and over. The ritual dagger was set on a round table near the bowl.

Nordvensen repeated the chant a good hundred times, then he paused and closed his eyes. The silence went on for a while. Suddenly I saw an image appear as if on a photographic paper immersed in a developing tank. It was Mona's image.

Nordvensen opened his eyes, seized the dagger, and slowly lifted it above his head. I stepped forward. Nordvensen uttered a terrible scream. The dagger was about to slash down toward Mona's face, when my leg sprang forward, up, turned. My foot caught him at the throat, he catapulted backward with his dagger, and Mona's image disappeared.

It took Nordvensen a few minutes to come to, and when he opened his eyes he was astonished to see me. He was scared. His eyes darted left and right, desperate for help. He sat up, massaging his windpipe, looking at the dagger that had gone flying across the room. I heard a rooster and noticed a birdcage.

"Let's go upstairs, Nordvensen. I don't like this room."

He had trouble breathing and stared at me with hallucinatory eyes. His voice was choked.

"To interrupt this ritual is a sacrilege that will bring Baron-Samedi's curse on you. You might have been the first noninitiate to attend an *envoi-mort* . . . You are fascinated by that . . . You are devoured by curiosity. You would like to know how such a thing is possible . . ."

"You are a sick man and a nut, Nordvensen."

"No jury would recognize me as such. You would subject yourself to ridicule."

"Who's talking about a jury?"

Nordvensen leaned forward. He picked up the dagger and went back to the bowl. I stood across from him, pulled out my gun, and pointed it between his eyes.

"Your weapons are powerless against mine. I send death spiritually and the spirit is faster than any bullet. Watch carefully, Zulu, because you are about to witness your own death. Isn't that the most fascinating show ever? I was on the verge of killing your girlfriend, but instead it will be your turn to be stabbed by the dagger and it is your blood that will color the water. But first, we need a sacrifice, an offering."

Transfixed by a morbid fascination, I let him go on. Realizing it, he went to the altar. He prayed standing up. He seemed to be holding some kind of conversation with the gods. He drank a little rum, lit a cigar. I watched him, fascinated. He didn't pay attention to me. After a few minutes he asked me to take the rooster from the cage and bring it to him. The rooster pecked me with its beak, making my hand bleed, but I grabbed it and brought it to Nordvensen, who held it expertly. With one swift stroke of the dagger, he cut the bird's head off and let the blood drip on himself while the decapitated fowl wildly beat his wings.

Nordvensen dropped the rooster, went back to the bowl and his litanies. I took up my place across from him and, like him, sweated profusely until my image appeared on the surface of the water. Nordvensen became silent. He stared at me; my eyes darted from him to the bowl.

He lifted the dagger and screamed, but the descent of the dagger was cut short by the .38 slug that smashed through his mouth, hurling him against the wall. My face vanished from the surface of the water, and I ran back upstairs, out of breath.

Laura was waiting for me, comfortably lounging in an armchair in the living room.

"You look a little pale, Zulu, dear."

"I almost witnessed my own death by voodoo."

"You should have called me."

"It's not really an entertainment."

"Where is the priest?"

"He is dead."

"I suppose one can kill oneself by mistake in these magic games."

"I helped him a little."

"I could use a strong drink."

"Help yourself. Pour one for me. I've got to call the cops."

There was a phone nearby. I dialed Brad's number.

"Hiya, copper."

"What's up, bro?"

"A corpse. Nordvensen. I had to shoot him. Self-defense."

"That's not your style."

"Nope."

"I'll call the New York police commissioner. You're in luck. He's a friend of mine."

"Thank God for the old-boys network . . . It was Nordvensen. I saw him at work. He was dispatching us into the other world."

"What do you mean 'us'?"

"Mona and me."

"Thank the Lord, I thought you were talking about me."

"Are you superstitious?"

"If you shot him, you must have had some doubts your own self."

"We all have our dark side."

"Weird . . . We'll have to talk about this . . ."

"Are you coming up?"

"I think I'd better."

"Don't call him right away. Give me time to go over the whole house."

"I am delighted to know you're finally seeing the light at the end of the tunnel."

"You bet . . ."

"Later, Zulu."

Nordvensen had an excellent bourbon. Laura and I paid our respects to it, then I settled down in the office of the captain without a ship to try to understand the torment of this lost soul.

"Can I go take a look?"

"If you want, but don't touch anything. Leaving finger-prints would only make things more complicated."

I started with the locked drawers. The keys were on the desk. Nordvensen was well organized. The files all had titles. One was labeled "Erwin." I pulled out a pile of letters. They were passionate love letters between him and Zab. Some letters were missing, no doubt those I had read at Parker's, selected because they had no references to Nordvensen. They were probably at police headquarters by now. The phone rang. I saw that the answering machine was turned on. I listened to the message.

"Everything's gone as planned. They've arrested Parker."

The caller hung up. It was probably a member of Nord-vensen's crackerjack team. I had to give them credit; they had managed to tail me without drawing my attention. Although it isn't hard when one has a big enough staff and a good organization.

Nordvensen's whole life had been focused on revenge after Erwin Zab's tragic demise. What was surprising was that Zab's love letters to Nordvensen were mixed with Nordvensen's love letters to him. He must have gotten them back after his lover-disciple's death. There were a number of photos, some taken against a background of exotic vegetation. Perhaps Haiti?

I went through piles of ordinary, uninteresting papers until I found two fascinating documents: bills from art galleries, one for a de Kooning, another one for a Joan Mitchell. To offer paintings like that to Rachel Zab, Nordvensen must have owed her a lot.

Laura stumbled back upstairs.

"You look pale, sweetie . . ."

She tried to smile, filling her glass with four fingers of bourbon and two ice cubes.

"It's horrible . . ."

It took me three hours to go over all the papers. I couldn't find any reference to Papa Mosso, but I was beginning to realize that the occult doesn't always leave traces.

"When the cops arrive, you don't know anything. You just drove me here, okay?"

"Okay. Are we going to be here a long time?"

"You can go home. I can get a ride from a friend who will be coming with the city police."

"I wouldn't mind getting out of here. I'm exhausted."

I walked her back to her car.

"Are you sure you can drive?"

"I'm okay."

"See you soon?"

"I promise."

I watched the taillights of the limo disappear into the night, took a deep breath of the sea air. The ocean had calmed down, which goes to prove that mythological clichés are not always accurate: powerful sorcerers can pass away without the elements turning wild. It reassured me, in a way, to realize that, given the right circumstances, one quickly becomes a believer.

I went back up to the villa, entering through the front gate. Since the house wasn't lit from this side, I followed the wall with my hand until I felt a fine engraving on the cornerstone. My fingers read a signature: Rachel Zab, 1976.

9

Brad, Lieutenant Cummings from the NYPD, a couple of ambulance drivers, and a bunch of local cops walked into the living room. I was asleep on the couch. Like all cops, they hadn't mastered the art of discreet entrance. Still, I had managed to sleep a couple of hours. Brad made the introductions. Cummings, a chubby little guy with the coloring of a salami, was trying to make a fashion statement with his black suit, bow tie, round glasses, and greased hair. I don't know how fresh and alert I looked, but he examined me with a certain curiosity. I was so used to working hand in hand with Brad that I tended to forget that most other cops don't like private detectives.

"Self-defense?" Cummings asked.

"He was going to stab me."

"Where did the bullet enter the body?"

"Through the mouth, came out through the neck."

"Why didn't you try to shoot him in the leg? That's what I call legitimate self-defense . . . At least, in the police force . . ."

"Do I have to remind you that we are investigating the death of a cop who tortured a suspect for a few hours until he died?" I said, putting a lid on his argument.

"Okay . . . Let's see the damage . . ."

"He's downstairs, in his voodoo temple," I told him, pointing to the staircase leading down from the office.

Brad lagged behind to talk to me.

"He's a friend, but take it easy, he has changed, he's not the same."

"Friends are like airplanes; you have to give them regular checkups."

"Okay, let's go . . ."

We went downstairs. Total silence awaited us. I must say the scene was interesting. Everything was exactly as I had left it, except for Nordvensen, who, though dead, must have gone to hell in his flesh and bones because he was nowhere to be found. He had left behind some debris of dark color, his clothes, his shoes. There was a bullet hole in the wall, fresh blood on the floor, plus the puddled blood of the sacrificed chicken, which had stayed behind.

After my brush with the voodoo world, I could believe that it was possible to kill one's victims from afar, but I found myself doubting this dead sorcerer had gone for a stroll on his own. All eyes were on me, expressions ranging from astonishment to the most intense displeasure.

"Okay, what's your explanation?"

"As Sherlock Holmes would say, hum . . . hum . . . hum . . . hum . . ."

"What about the dagger he tried to stab you with?"

"He must have taken it with him."

"What can happen to a man who gets shot in the mouth by a .38 bullet and walks away?"

"He's going to have serious problems swallowing."

Brad looked distraught. Cummings was turning purple. I made an effort and told them what had happened in detail, although I kept some of the information I had found in Nordvensen's papers to myself.

Cummings listened with attention, then sent a cop to inspect the stairs, three others to search the house, while the remaining ones took pictures and picked up bits of ectoplasm off the floor and walls. The forensic guy who was in charge of the harvesting agreed to give me one of his little plastic bag. They also found some traces of blood, as though the body had been dragged.

"He must have crawled out of here."

I could tell Cummings couldn't stand me anymore, but sometimes I couldn't help pushing things. It was impossible to find any trace of footprints in the sand because the violent wind coming off the ocean would have filled them. We went upstairs and conferred in the living room.

"Technically, if there's no body, there's no death. All I can do is declare Nordvensen missing."

"So, you too believe in magic?"

"Brad," Cummings yelled, "tell me again why you're protecting this asshole."

Brad didn't get upset by this.

"He is the best detective I know, and he's very tight with the district attorney's office . . . Also, he usually finds what he's looking for."

"Okay . . . I am going back to New York City, but I'll wait

to hear from you. I'll arrange to have the beach searched and I'll send the dogs. You can keep the leftovers."

"Yeah, who knows, he could be hiding in the sand."

Cummings got up, nodded to Brad, and left with his crew without saying good-bye to me. He made me think of a shabby theater director trying to make something out of an avant-garde play. Just as he was leaving, I couldn't resist warning him:

"Watch out, you might inadvertently step on Nord-vensen out there. His dagger would slice through your Italian shoes like butter."

He didn't answer. I offered a drink to Brad. I knew I had made things difficult for him.

"This whole story is unbelievable."

"The only thing I can think of is that Nordvensen's people came to get him while I was asleep."

"But why wouldn't they kill you?"

"If I had opened an eye, I bet I would have seen the bullet on its way to my brain."

I poured myself a drink too. The day was dawning, the ocean calm.

"I think they came for his body. They probably wanted to give him a big voodoo funeral, maybe hide his grave in order to make it a gathering place where they could practice their black magic."

"Maybe," Brad said. "I had Parker arrested, as you asked. Everything went fine."

"I know. I got the message from one of Nordvensen's assistants."

"So, do you think we'll ever find the body?"

"No. It's just like in the movies, *The Return of the Living Dead II*."

"Do you have any proof?"

"Tons of it."

I took Brad to the office, showed him the files I had put aside.

"It's weird that they didn't clean out the place."

"Lack of time."

Brad took the files. He walked around the house, gathering any of Nordvensen's leftovers that might be construed as evidence.

"I'll leave the blood and the chicken for Cummings," Brad said. "We have enough evidence to close the case."

"I am surprised I can't find the master tapes."

"Are you sure there's no safe?"

"Positive."

I filled Brad in on the rest of the story on our way back to the city. I was convinced Clementine would find out Nordvensen had been a disciple of Papa Mosso and that he had used his evil power to obtain revenge. The only thing I didn't understand was the connection between Princess Bashma and Nordvensen. Okay, so maybe she had compromising documents in her possession, but they could have gotten them without murdering her. True, her new album, *Pure Steel,* was going to have allusions to Kate's father but, frankly, I couldn't see any rap fan having the curiosity to ask questions about it. The lyrics would have simply sounded antiracist. Maybe there was still something more to figure out in this strange story.

I asked Brad to pull up at a convenience store to buy sandwiches and coffee. I was starved.

"I can close this case whether we find Nordvensen or not. That way you won't have any more dealings with Cummings."

"Okay, go ahead, close it . . . But I want to keep fooling around a little more, just for the kick of it . . ."

"Suit yourself. Want to go fishing for a couple of days?"

"Anytime."

"We could go down to the Keys and rent a boat there. But just the two of us. If we invite Joe, he's bound to show up with some S&M chick and then call us to remove the hook from his dick . . . I'm worried about him . . . He's getting too far out there . . . And we need him as DA. Did you know that according to our polls, he's the front-runner?"

"I didn't know you took polls?"

"Now and then. The police are interested in a lot of things . . . It's the media that scares me. And his chicks. One of these days one of them is going to try to blackmail him."

"You'll take care of that."

"I've got to be careful. I've got my share of enemies in the department."

"Do you want me to make him quit the hard stuff?"

Brad laughed.

"You're kidding!"

"No . . . If I sent him a girl with a good script that we would figure out together and if he really got scared, maybe he would stop, but we would need a really smart girl, and we shouldn't be afraid to push it really far."

"You always have brilliant ideas, Zulu."

"He would have to be more scared than sexually aroused."

We left the car at JFK and caught the first flight out to Miami. I was eager to be in Mona's arms; my cells craved the tender feel of her skin and the creative improvisations of her lips.

This time I didn't bring anything back for Live Crew. Brad dropped me off at the Palace. He promised to have the specimens in the plastic bag analyzed. I ordered a grilled Bora Bora with a bottle of Chablis, followed by chocolate cake and an espresso, sniffed the attar of Miami in little greedy breaths, and

topped the feast with a Churchill brought by my fairy god-
mother. She agreed to eat an ice cream in my company. Gloria
hadn't started her shift yet. Someone else brought me my mail.
There were the usual bills that I handed over to my bookkeeper
every two weeks to write the checks. I had the delicious surprise
to find a beautiful red envelope containing a few lines written by
Mona, penciled on a piece of paper tablecloth:

> *Zulu, little bugger,*
> *My skin screams,*
> *My body shakes,*
> *I am waiting for you,*
> *Naked and perfumed*
> *With the jasmine*
> *That you love so well.*
> *Mona*

It was fresh and pretty. I kept the poem and the envelope. I booked a hotel room, took a long shower, lay down for
fifteen minutes under the fan to dry myself, slipped twenty dollars to the doorman who was reading a study on serial killers
. . . and walked to Beach Pressing to change clothes. To celebrate
my resurrection, I picked out a suit of a tropical cream color and
a fifties tie, sky blue with yellow circles and red triangles. I
completed the look with socks printed with saguaro cactuses
and a pair of night blue Rossetti sandals.

I took my bathing suit with me, went down to the beach,
swam three miles, and met a gorgeous athlete who gave me a
membership card for an aerobics club that met on the beach
every evening at nine.

"You have a great body but you could still improve your
definition."

I talked with her for a couple of minutes before calling
Live Crew. They met me at the beach a few minutes later.

"Give me a complete report, kids . . ."

"We missed you a lot," Roy told me.

"It's true," Lita added.

That adoring welcome left me speechless.

"Well, you almost lost your jobs, guys."

"What would happen in that case?" Lita asked.

"I've left instructions with my lawyer. You would get the
car, a nice little bundle of dough, and a picture of me as a babe
that you could frame and proudly display on your fireplace."

"Maybe it'd be worth getting rid of him," Roy ventured
with a beautiful smile.

"Not a bad idea," Lita added.

She went on with her report.

"No news from Clementine. Roy is beginning to understand he doesn't have to fuck me so hard I bang my head against
the wall each time he pushes his dick inside me, and . . ."

"But that's how they do it in the movies," Roy defended
himself, "and I swear there are girls who like that . . ."

"Young and impetuous . . ." I started with philosophy.

"Thanks for that wisdom, old master."

"Listen to this . . ."

Roy popped Roxanne Shanté's latest in the blaster. She
was chilling.

"It's a present from us."

We stretched on the sand like alligators, watching the
sun dive into the ocean, then walked to the Fontainebleau to
finish off the evening.

"Are you inviting us to dinner?" Lita asked with an irresistible smile.

We sat down in the shade of a palm. After I gave them

the green light, they picked the most expensive items on the menu. I believed in treating my staff decently. Around midnight we went to the Club Nu, decorated with a bunch of dragons hanging from the ceiling and featuring a band of girl rockers from California, Concrete Blonds, who made us dance till five A.M., quitting time for Mona.

I headed straight for her pimp, Sweetie Pie Speed. It was time to make a deal with him. I parked behind his car and invited myself into his palatial ride. He slapped my hand with the beatific smile of the mack who smells the blues.

"Hey, man, are you coming to talk business?"

"Yep."

"Looks like Mona's pussy really turns you on."

"I want to buy her from you."

"What's your pleasure, my man? A joint? A hit? Some scotch?"

"Scotch."

He handed me a flask that was lying on the leather seat. I took a couple of swigs.

"She's my main girl, do you know that? It takes six months of hard work to train a bitch, not mentioning all the losers that just suck up your dough . . . The junkies, the mentally unstable, those who are always in and out of the hospital. That's not Mona. Mona's a queen."

"That's why I am here. Name your price."

"Thirty grand sounds reasonable to me. Cheap, even."

I slapped him on the back, laughed noisily, and got out of the car. I walked back toward Mona. I heard the heavy door of the Lincoln Continental, like the sound of a fat fish diving into a lagoon. Sweetie Pie Speed caught up with me.

"Is that above your means? I heard you made a bundle."

"Good reason not to throw it out the window."

"Don't you think the pussy is worth it?"

"Nope."

"How much is it worth, in your opinion?"

"Seventeen grand, cash, tomorrow."

"Go fuck yourself, motherfucker. Fifteen is the price of pussy that has more miles than a 747. Pussies on Grand Avenue cost that much. Do your shopping over there."

"Those pussies are worth five thousand on the financial market."

Sweetie Pie Speed laughed.

"Do you have financial counsel?"

"I've got friends."

"Where would you have her work?"

"Privately."

"Yeah. You'd better. If you take her, I don't want to see her around here no more. I would lose money. I can give you credit. Let's say fifteen tomorrow and a thousand a week for eighteen weeks."

"For your information, that amounts to thirty-three thousand."

"That's the price of credit these days."

"Damnit, I feel like I'm talking to my banker."

"And she still works for me until she's all paid up."

"I think you're doing too well, Speed. I don't see you willing to negotiate. I'll have to find myself another bitch. I'll spend one last night with the kid, and then she's all yours."

Speed lit up a joint.

"After all," I added, "Paradise City is full of foxy little numbers you can buy with dinner at Burger King and a little bit of know-how."

Speed let his joint die, laboring under the stress of seeing a bundle of instant cash vanish into thin air.

"Ciao, Speed."

He didn't answer but watched me go over to Mona, who had been following the scene while keeping her cool. Only her eyes were glittering like pieces of mica. We got back into my car. I pulled up near Speed, she tossed him the money she owed him, and we took off.

Mona rubbed against me. My wiring lit up like the laser beams that sweep through the sky of Miami at night.

"I missed you, Zulu."

"I missed you too, Mona. I feel dry like a mummy when you're not with me."

"Is he going to do it?"

"He'll do it before dawn."

"Are we going to a hotel?"

"No, let's go to your place. I have a feeling he'll come over to close the deal before daybreak."

"I don't want to give him more than twenty grand."

"I'm the one who's going to be forking the dough, baby."

"No, I don't want to owe anybody anything no more. It's not a good way to start."

"As you like it."

"I put a bottle of champagne to chill."

"Good girl!"

Half sitting, half lying down on her sofa, we watched the night, sniffing it, while our skins became reacquainted.

"I want to fuck you, Zulu."

We went inside. Drums made a little room for us on the bed. Mona undressed me.

"Don't move . . . It's my solo . . . Let me do it."

I laughed. Mona slid against me like a cool breeze. She touched my whole body in slow caresses. I felt her dense and tender breasts graze my feet, my thighs, my groin, my stomach, my chest, my throat, my face. Every one of my cells got turned on. I licked the breasts as they came and went over me. Her whole body seemed to be hanging from invisible strings. I lost all notion of time, I was tingling all over, the energy surging up and down my body. Her tongue, her lips, her teeth were gently biting into my flesh. I couldn't move anymore, I felt crucified by an interminable ecstasy.

The birds started to sing. We were pressed against each other, trying to connect each square inch of skin. I had the acute feeling that Speed was sitting on the sofa, watching us. We had to play it close to the vest. I winked at Mona, pointing toward the inside of the house with my chin. I got up, got dressed.

"Are you leaving?"

"Yo, gorgeous. I had a bitching time with you."

"Do you mean you're splitting for good?"

"Yep. I think we've gone as far as we are going to go, you and I."

"You're all the same. When your dick is satisfied, you turn into ghosts."

"What did you think, that we would go around the world together?"

"Listen, asshole, I've been around more than you think. Get out, motherfucker."

"Here, take this bill. It wasn't worth more than that."

Mona tossed a lamp in my direction; it crashed against the wall. I heard Speed leave discreetly. Mona had been perfect. I kissed her and went out.

I walked a few hundred yards. The white ocean liner was following me. Speed finally passed me and signaled me to stop.

He looked really upset.

"We've got to talk seriously, Zulu."

"We've already talked."

"Shit, you're not a real African, are you? You don't appreciate the joys of haggling."

"There comes a point when the deal cools off."

"Don't believe that, man . . . Nobody likes business as much as I do . . . We've got to be a little more understanding of each other, that's all . . ."

"So?"

"You started too low . . . You've got to take into account the real market value of a product. You know what the kid can do . . . If you set her up with a phone line, in a nice studio, that bitch is a high-class pussy . . . All you gotta do is give her a little polish . . . dress her upscale . . ."

"You know how much a studio costs right now?"

"Twenty grand."

"I'm talking Miami Beach, man . . . At least three times that . . ."

"Don't be a dog, Zulu, you want to bleed me?"

"You've got to take the opportunity when it comes."

"Give me a price . . . Cash . . ."

"Twenty . . ."

"Thirty, she's yours. You can have her right now."

"I am making an offer, the last one. After that, you'll never see me again."

"You're a tough businessman, mister."

"Twenty-two. Tomorrow night."

Speed smiled sadly, as if I were tearing his heart out.

"Okay . . . You're making the best deal of the decade . . ."

"You'll be able to buy a new set of wheels . . ."

"Why, what's the matter with my car?"

"I wonder if it'll pass the next inspection."

"Tomorrow . . . Used bills, not freshly printed dough."

"Tomorrow."

I couldn't go back to Mona's. I drove straight to Miami Beach, took a quiet room, and fell asleep like a newborn babe.

Around three P.M. I showed up at the Palace, where Gloria greeted me with a relaxed smile.

"You look fresh as a rose."

"I stopped by yesterday . . ."

"That's what I heard . . ."

"Give me an extra muffin, I'm starved."

She poured my coffee, I petted her a little, she came back with my mail. There was a Federal Express envelope. I opened it. To tell you the truth, my blood pressure shot straight up. Inside was a letter and the Polaroid I had left at Nordvensen's, as signature. I immediately recognized the handwriting. It was the first time a dead man had written to me and the message wasn't particularly pleasant:

Hello, young innocent one. I warned you, your weapons are terribly material. It is probably the last time you will use them. Mona is going to die gently, and then it will be your turn. I will use the soft method. It takes a long time and it's incredibly painful. Welcome to hell.

Gloria was laughing when she came back; she was practically dancing with my plate. She stopped dead in her tracks when she saw my face.

"What's wrong?"

"I think you can bring all that back to the kitchen."

"It's the first time I've seen a letter spoil your appetite."

She kissed me to make me feel better. I called Live Crew, chewed on a muffin. They came in a hurry. The phone whistled. It was Brad.

"I've got the lab results. The bag contained fragments of

human lungs, spleen, and liver. The blood group is the same as the blood and the pieces of brain that were found on the wall."

"You make me feel a little better."

"You sound weird. Is there a problem?"

"I just got a letter from Nordvensen, Federal Express."

Brad thought that was very funny.

"You're getting fucking superstitious, man. I thought Nordvensen was counting grains of sand in the great beyond."

"Maybe," I said.

"No question about it. Do you want me to stop by?"

"Don't bother. I'm trying to get back into the swing of things around here."

"Parker is safe," Brad said. "I talked to him this morning. He's fine."

"It's nice to know that some people are doing fine. Okeydokey, catch you later."

Live Crew was starved. I took my phone and went for a walk on the beach to invoke Exu, hoping to hear from Clementine. I waited almost two hours. I called Brad back, asked him for Parker's phone number, called Parker up and filled him in on the whole story.

"Do you believe that if he set these forces in motion before he died, they would take effect postmortem?"

"If he had done that job, he wouldn't have had to use the clay bowl."

"Good point."

"Remember, such a traditional job can be undone by a number of voodoo priests. Clementine can do it."

"I wish I'd hear from her."

"Don't worry, Zulu. You're safe."

"Is it possible that pieces of dried-up organs can be used to undo a spell?"

"In my opinion, they don't belong to Nordvensen."

"Same blood group."

"A lot of people belong to the same group."

"It's true."

"Would you have a picture of Nordvensen, by any chance, and a piece of clothing?"

"The police have that . . . I can get it right away."

"Good."

I drove straight to Brad's, picked up a shirt stained with blood, a piece of dehydrated liver, and a photo. That would be enough to work with.

I don't know if Exu had heard me, but the good Clementine called me up. She was at the airport with first-class info.

The BMW roared, I stopped by at the bank, picked up twenty-two grand, and got to the airport in less than twelve minutes, thanks to a police motorcade that opened the way for me.

Clementine had the happy look of someone who's found a treasure. I kissed her.

"It hasn't been easy, but I found what I was looking for."

"You are wonderful, Clementine."

We were walking toward my car. I was carrying her little old leather suitcase.

"Papa Mosso had a daughter, Eurydice. She lives where, in your opinion?"

"In Miami?" I ventured, not quite sure of my answer.

"Exactly."

"Do you have her address?"

"Yes."

"Recent?"

"Yes, I got it through one of her nieces."

"You have the soul of a real detective."

"I didn't want to let you spend all that money for nothing."

"Does she practice voodoo?"

"No, she gave it up. She married a car dealer twelve years ago."

"I hope she'll know something."

"From what I have heard, her father had great hopes for her. He initiated her and for years she was part of his *humfo*."

Clementine rummaged through her pockets and pulled out a piece of brown paper on which was scribbled Eurydice's address.

10

Eurydice lived in a low ranch house, five cars from the fifties parked out front and no husband in sight. The lawn looked as if it was mowed every week. No tree interrupted the straight lines. An open garage, a car with its hood propped up, tools. Fred—that was the husband's name—must have been into car restoration. I decided to go in alone. Clementine understood, although she was dying of curiosity.

I rang the bell, a dog barked. A woman's voice made him stop. Eurydice glanced at me through the glass door and decided that I was neither a door-to-door salesman nor a robber. She opened the door.

She was a handsome woman of about fifty, standing very straight. She had a curved nose, very black skin, intelligent eyes.

"Eurydice Gonzales?"

"Yes, it's me."

"I am a detective. I would like to speak to you."

She looked slightly worried.

"Something happened to my son?"

"No, don't worry."

She was wearing a cotton dress and an apron that she took off. She had flour on her hands.

"Come in. I was baking a cake."

"With orange flower . . ."

She laughed.

"You have a good nose . . ."

The inside of the house was comfortably furnished. The colors of the wall-to-wall carpeting, the chairs, the sofa, in different shades of faded chamomile, were not very attractive. Only the curtains, printed with little red and blue flowers, brought some life.

"Sit down, sir . . ."

"My name is Zulu."

"Is it your real name?"

"No, my name is Ignazio Talawapi Alónzo Marwin Utusha Tenero."

"Oh, I see."

I sat down in one of the huge armchairs.

"I just made a pitcher of lime juice, would you care for some?"

"With pleasure."

I heard a refrigerator spit out some ice cubes into glasses. She came back, sat down, and dried her hands on her dress. Eurydice had a narrow waist and very wide hips. Painted in blue she would have looked like a Matisse.

"Does your husband fix old cars?"

"No, he has a Toyota dealership. It's my son, Luis. There is a good market for them. He redoes everything, including the leather. It's a lot of work, at least three months per car."

"I might be interested in one, at some point."

"You know where to find him."

"You are the only person who can help me . . . Maybe the only one who can save my life . . ."

She looked surprised. But her face was not devoid of compassion and I started to feel better.

"What's it about?"

"I am investigating a case involving voodoo. Five persons have met inexplicable death. The man who is responsible for these deaths, according to my deductions, must have been a disciple of your father. We haven't been able to identify him, although we have some leads . . . Since I am the next on his list I am working very hard to crack this case . . . You see, I love life . . ."

Eurydice's face had become serious and sad; images must have been running through her memory.

"I hoped my father had died taking with him the ultimate secrets of his diabolical art . . . Can you describe precisely how these people passed on?"

I described it the best I could, and she had to agree that these were not your garden variety *envois-morts*.

"From what you are saying, this very well could be the way my father worked . . ."

"Did you ever attend his ceremonies?"

"My father initiated me into the voodoo world when I was very young and I had strong powers, but before we get into that, you've got to understand something . . . At the age of seventeen, I had a kind of vision that definitively took me away from voodoo. I stayed alone in a cabin for more than a year

. . . I purified myself from the baleful universe in which I had lived and I drifted away from my father, who became very sad because of that. If he had wanted to use his powers to fight evil, he would have been a great man . . ."

Eurydice looked away for a while, then continued:

"Papa Mosso had been perverted when he was very young by a voodoo priest who had adopted him. My family had been massacred by landowners who had taken our land, and my father had the duty to revenge his brothers, his sisters, and his parents. There was terrible hate in his heart . . . But for me there was nobody to take revenge on. Those who had hurt us were dead. The cycle was closed. We were not able to regain our plantation . . . It was too late, but my father had only learnt one thing . . . the most terrible violence . . ."

"But you could have reversed that force and used it to save human lives . . ."

She smiled sadly. My suggestion must have seemed naive to her.

"In order to do that, one must return the *envois-morts* and kill the one who has sent it. There is no difference, in spite of what people think, between white magic and black magic. All magic touches evil, at one point . . . If I had wanted to save lives, I would have had to engage in a magical war with the most powerful voodoo priest, my father, and I would have died, like all those who had confronted him . . . I had only one solution . . . Christ saved me from this world . . ."

"I understand . . . Did your father have many disciples?"

"His *humfo* was very popular . . ."

"Did you know them all?"

"Yes, I think so . . . Most of them died tragically . . . They didn't have his black power . . ."

Eurydice became very emotional. I gently prodded her to go on.

"In a certain way . . . I killed my father . . . When I came out of isolation, he didn't ask me any questions . . . He immediately saw that I had found the light . . . that the light was infallible . . . He died three months later . . . He had no successor . . ."

I was moved too. I drank a little. I showed her Nordvensen's photo.

"Nord," she said, with a smile that was half sad, half amused.

"Do you think your father might have taught him the method of killing one's victim by conjuring his image on water and stabbing it with a dagger?"

Eurydice laughed sadly.

"He was very rich, but my father always made fun of him. He said he would never have the gift, the force. He kept teaching him, because Nord paid him very well. He even bought a beautiful house for my father."

I was amazed by what I had just learned.

"Are you sure he couldn't have made progress by himself, or with somebody else's help?"

"A person's latent power can be felt immediately. As soon as you see somebody you can tell what they'll be able to accomplish and what they won't, even after ten or twenty years of intense practice."

"He was my principal suspect."

"He was a proud and intelligent man. He liked the game of voodoo. He loved drama but he would not have been capable of the slightest magical act. I know he also practiced hypnosis to convince people of his power."

I couldn't believe that the image that appeared on the surface of the water was due to suggestion, but, on the other hand, I had trouble thinking that Eurydice's judgment might be at fault.

"Did Papa Mosso have other disciples who might have mastered his method?"

"Yes, but, as I told you, they are all dead."

"During the year that you lived in solitude, your father might have had another disciple whom you might not have met."

"I would have heard about him . . . My father would have told me . . . Anyway, at the end of his life, he wasn't practicing much anymore. He had found other pleasures . . ."

"Such as?"

Eurydice laughed, she seemed embarrassed.

"He had fallen in love with a girl, younger than myself. A very beautiful American girl. She must have been around fifteen. She lived with my father till the end."

"What was her name?"

"Princess."

"Do you mean to say she actually had royal blood?"

"No . . . People called her that . . . I never knew her real name . . ."

All of a sudden a circuit lit up in my head, all the wires connected. Thanks to the books, thanks to my built-in hard drive that stored so much information: Princess was the name of the heroine in *Sweet Bird of Youth,* the Tennessee Williams play in which Erwin Zab had been playing the part of Chance at the time he was killed by Henning. Princess could only be Rachel Zab. I was dumbstruck.

"Are you all right?" Eurydice asked me.

"Yes . . . Can you describe her to me?"

"She was rather tall for her age, black hair, beautiful eyes. She had a tragic and vibrant look that must have seduced my father."

I imagined Rachel at fifteen, wild with rage after the death of her brother, ready to do anything to take her revenge.

Nordvensen, whom she knew, must have acted the part of the big voodoo priest, and through Nordvensen she must have met Papa Mosso.

"Is it possible for a very gifted young woman to learn how to send *envois-morts* in fifteen months?"

"Your question upsets me . . . I am thinking that my father must have been terribly disappointed to lose me . . . It is possible that he transferred all of his hopes to Princess and that he initiated her into his most secret rituals . . . . It is not a question of age but of force, and now that I think about it, it is true that a special force emanated from Princess."

I was transfixed by what I had just realized, by the power of the hate that Princess felt for the world, by the extraordinary cunning she had displayed. Indeed, she went on manipulating Nordvensen exactly the same way as Papa Mosso had done it, to get money out of him. I hadn't been able to fool her with Parker's false arrest, and the sign, a distortion of the infinity symbol, now seemed an obvious choice.

"I believe that you saved my life, Eurydice. I know Princess and she is certainly the authoress of these crimes. Only one thing intrigues me. Why didn't she send you death, since you are the only link that connects her with Papa Mosso?"

"I know the secrets, and if I were threatened, I would feel it immediately. Death would boomerang right back to the sender and would destroy her instantly."

"I have a technical question . . . If Princess were to be arrested, isolated, would she still be able to send death?"

"The ritual is merely a support of the strength of the spirit, but it is important nevertheless. In the *envois-morts* my father used to practice, it was the clay bowl that mattered. It has to be made by the priest in a very specific way: physical elements of the victims, like a piece of clothing, hair and nail clippings, must be incorporated within the clay, and the clay must be left to dry in the sun for three days and then be exposed to the moon for one night."

"Princess possesses these elements. Someone took the clippings and the clothing from me and my friend."

"So there is only one thing to do, you must find the clay bowls and destroy them by dissolving them in spring water."

"But what if she is still in possession of the nail clippings and the hair?"

"She will need three days and one night to make another bowl."

"I am confronted by a terrible dilemma: How can I save myself, and those who are destined to die with me?"

"I know a man who might be able to help you. He is very powerful. Even my father feared him. He lives in Jamaica and goes by the name of Clesh. You will find him near a village called Black River."

Still shaky, I smiled.

"He has already failed twice against Princess."

"Maybe at the time he didn't know where the *envoi-mort* was coming from."

I got up, kissed Eurydice. Just when I was about to leave, she called me back, looked deep into my eyes, and told me:

"To erase the evil that my father has done, I am ready to lose my soul. I will go to Jamaica with you."

A car pulled up. A man walked toward the house.

"It's my husband. Let me handle it."

"Fred, this is Mr. Marwin, from the *Miami Herald* . . ."

"Hi, nice to meet you."

He shook my hand.

"Do you remember the contest?"

"Yes . . . Yes . . ."

"Well, guess what? I won! One week in Jamaica, all expenses paid. I am leaving tomorrow."

"Everything will be ready, madam. I will come myself to pick you up with the ticket."

Eurydice had a true gift for improvisation. I left feeling that maybe I had a future after all, which was kind of refreshing. I knew we were not eternal, but we might as well be eternal as long as possible.

I got back into the car with Clementine and Live Crew. It looked as if I was about to jump into yet another plane. This was an emergency. I had to save Mona's soul and mine too. There's something strange about finding yourself captured whole in a bowl of clay dried by the sun and the moon. Science has its plus sides, but sometimes it is completely deficient.

"So?" Clementine asked. She was dying with curiosity.

"Maybe I have a chance for survival."

"Too bad," commented Roy.

I slapped him upside the head.

"Clementine, would you like to spend a couple of days in Miami? Live Crew will take good care of you. You will have a beautiful room on the ocean. They'll take you to good restaurants, read to you, take you dancing. Roy will walk on his hands for you and they will introduce you to dragons."

"What an itinerary . . . Yes, I accept . . ."

"Okay, I am on my way to Atlanta. I'll be back tonight or first thing in the morning."

I tossed a wad of bills to Lita.

"Make yourselves happy."

"You are truly turning into a three-star establishment, Zulu," Lita said, sitting behind the wheel.

"Do you know what I'm building?" Roy asked.

"I have no idea."

"A motor-powered scooter. It goes up to sixty miles per hour."

"Really?"

"It's true," Lita said. "I rode it."

"I didn't know you were into that kind of thing . . . If I'm not back by five in the morning, give this envelope to Sweetie Pie Speed, will you?"

I handed it to Lita. She hefted it.

"Hmmm . . . He'll be able to open a supermarket . . . Do you need a receipt?"

"The receipt is his life. He knows it . . . I hope . . ."

Clementine was laughing. She was in another world.

"I'd love to go dancing tonight."

"Don't worry, Grandma," Roy said respectfully, "we'll blast you right up to cloud nine."

At the airport, I asked Lita to reserve three seats on a flight to Kingston tomorrow. One for Eurydice, one for Mona, one for me.

"Shall I get return tickets?"

"No, I'm getting superstitious."

"When you get back, are you going to tell us everything?" Clementine asked.

"Every detail."

As usual, I got into the plane just when the doors were closing. A charming stewardess brought me a split of Veuve Clicquot. A young woman saw me walk by and changed seats to sit next to me.

"Excuse me, sir . . . Your face seems so reassuring . . . I am terrified of flying . . . Do you mind if I sit next to you?"

She looked about thirty. Gray suit, blue eyes, blond hair, a voice vibrant with fear, a gray crocodile bag, matching pumps, a little diamond, a wedding band. Nice tits and ass. I was not going to refuse to console an attractive phobic like that.

"Sit back, deep into the seat . . . Right, just like that . . ."

I fastened her seat belt. I placed my right hand on her solar plexus. She didn't wear a bra.

"Breathe slowly and deeply . . . That's it . . ."

She was gasping, but the heat of my hand relaxed her and she glanced at me with gratitude. I had already read the airline safety instructions many times and I felt perfectly suited for any first-aid emergency. A Texan whose hands were covered with turquoise stones set in solid silver rings stared at me with unbridled hate. He would have loved to be in my shoes.

"Oh my God, the plane is moving . . . ," the blond whispered in panic.

"A triple bourbon," I requested from the stewardess, who, understanding the situation, served us before we took off.

I gave the drink to my pretty little blond baby. What a good wet nurse I was! The Swiss should hire me as a Saint Bernard.

"A prince must save a princess locked in a Moorish palace. A eunuch keeps watch over her. He is armed with a machete, and the prince wanders into a labyrinth full of dragons. Trapdoors spiked with steel nails open, the prince avoids the last trap by leaping out of the way, but a dragon rushes forward and—"

"The plane is moving faster . . ."

"Yes, and the dragon opens his wings and flies over the prince, who pulls out his gold and emerald sword and shouts. Meanwhile, the dragon spews terrible flames that singe the prince's eyebrows . . ."

During my improvisation, I gently massaged her stomach up to her breasts. She could barely breathe.

"Breathe, Princess, breathe . . ."

She sucked in a thimble's worth of pressurized air; her temples were covered with sweat. The plane took off, and she screamed and took me in her arms. I stroked her face and her hair. Her lips were stiff with fear; I licked them to help her relax. The princess dug her nails into the soft fabric of my suit while the plane climbed toward the sky. Her whole body was shaking. I kissed her more savagely and, since she couldn't breathe for a good minute, she had to gulp for breath. The Texan was staring at us with his beady black eyes in which was burning a Ku Klux Klan cross. That guy was going to lynch me as soon as he could unfasten his seat belt. He was crimson with hate, about to explode.

While the plane was climbing, I slipped one hand on my beautiful traveling companion's left breast, went on kissing her, and noticed with pleasure that her tongue was softening and wrapping itself around mine. The princess opened her legs, holding back deep and soft moans. Her left leg came over mine. I stroked her nape and ear, kissed her neck. My hand slipped, followed the delicate line of her stocking all the way to the strap of the garter belt. I pulled her panties aside, gently stroked her wet and burning sex. The princess started to undulate like the dragon in my story. Her screams were filling the first-class cabin. The Texan would have already shot me if the ground control were not so strict. I blessed the security services. The captain's deep and sonorous voice came on in the cabin:

"Hi, guys. We have reached our cruising altitude of twenty-seven thousand feet. The slight turbulence you've been feeling is due to the mass of warm air coming in contact with colder currents, but I think from now on we'll have a very good flight. The temperature in Atlanta is one hundred and eight degrees Fahrenheit . . . Don't hesitate to call our stewardesses if there is anything we can do to make your flight more pleasant. We know you have the choice between a number of airlines and we thank you for choosing Delta. Our landing is due in fifty-eight minutes and I wish you a pleasant flight."

The princess came with a long scream. The stewardess rushed to our seats, looked at us with compassion. I clicked open our seat belts and the stewardess opened the way for us to the toilets like a motorcade. The sick blond princess pretended to hold back a flow threatening to gush out from her entrails, but once we were alone in the peace of the tiny love chamber, we got undressed completely. Although short-term, the therapy seemed to work, and the blond princess covered my whole body with her inflamed tongue. I noticed with pleasure that blonds, too, could show taste and artistry. She came again between my lips. I came in her mouth. We furiously made love while she was leaning against the sink, and a last orgasm made us scream together at the very moment the Boeing hit the ground.

We got dressed while the plane was taxiing toward the gate. The blond princess, her eyes all lit up, laughed while she touched up her makeup. I heard the passengers get out of the plane, and when everything seemed silent, we carefully opened the door. To our greatest surprise, the whole crew was waiting for us and we deplaned under a storm of applause.

We were walking very tropically on the carpet of black rubber. The blond princess looked at me, discreetly winked, then walked faster. I watched her swinging shape move thirty feet ahead of me. When she came out into the airport lobby, a tall blond guy, athletic and elegant, took her in his arms. I heard this dialogue between them:

"The trip wasn't too hard on you, was it, honey?"

"It was great. I'll never be afraid of flying again."

"I told you the therapy would work . . ."

I walked another few dozen feet. The Texan, purple with rage, was waiting for us. I thought he would come to me, but he approached the happy couple and I heard him yell at the tall blond guy:

"Mister, your wife is nothing but a cheap whore!"

This was the end of the conversation, for the tall blond guy punched him in the face and knocked him out flat. He smiled to the princess, and they both walked past me.

"Who's that nut?" asked the handsome husband.

"He was sitting next to me. He tried to take advantage of a moment of panic."

The beautiful princess and her prince charming strolled away. The Texan still hadn't moved. A steward was courteously slapping him to help him come to.

When I emerged from the airport I felt cool as a cucumber. What was awaiting me was a little heavier. I took a cab to Rachel Zab's, a very different kind of princess. On the way, feeling hungry, I asked the driver to stop at a Burger King drive-in. I ordered a double bacon cheeseburger.

"You eat that junk food?" the driver asked me.

"Occasionally. It's delicious."

"I heard it makes hair grow in your ears."

"Who told you that?"

"My wife. She works in a health food store."

"I don't have any hair in my ears yet."

"My wife tells me you are what you eat."

"If I turn into a hamburger before we get to my destination, would you be kind enough to drive me to a hospital and ask the surgeon to first remove the slices of bacon? Otherwise, it might be disorienting for the people who have to do business with me."

"Are you in the movies?"

"Yeah."

"Actor?"

"No, dialogue coach."

He pulled up in front of the glass door of the beautiful black building. The ravishing secretary seemed thrilled to see me. She was wearing a yellow miniskirt and was about to leave. I realized it was closing time for the office.

"Hi, is Rachel here?"

"I didn't know you were going to stop by. She is with a client, but I'll tell her you are here."

"Do you know if she is doing anything tonight?"

"No, I don't think so."

"Wonderful, I'll be able to invite her for dinner."

"Would you like a scotch or some coffee?"

"Coffee, please."

I sat down. The secretary came back with a cup. She had beautiful eyebrows almost touching each other.

"Did you make a decision for your villa?"

"Yes, I am getting close . . ."

"Glad to hear it. Sugar?"

"Thank you."

She stirred, handed me the cup, her face close to mine. She seemed surprised, laughed.

"What's the matter?"

"Nothing . . . Nothing . . ." she said, blushing a bit.

I realized I still smelled of the blond princess's delicious odor.

"It's new. Very expensive."

"Really? What's it called?"

"Pussy, by Chanel."

She laughed out loud.

"Are you staying in town tonight?"

"I don't know yet."

"There's a convention. It's going to be hard to find a room."

She peeled a sky blue Post-it from a pad on the desk and wrote a number on it. She gave it to me with a dazzling smile.

"If you come, I'll cover you with rose petals . . ."

"Hmmmm . . ."

"My name is Fiona . . ."

She disappeared, leaving me with the delicious thoughts of rose petals and organ music.

Rachel walked her client to the door. From the looks of him, he was very satisfied. She locked the door and came to me with a big smile, bigger than the last time.

"I wanted to thank you," I told her. "You've been wonderful. Without you, I wouldn't have been able to find the murderer."

"I did what I could, in memory of Erwin."

"Are you free tonight?"

"Yes. I was thinking of going to the movies, but that can wait."

"I have a proposal for you. I want to call the best caterer in town and have a delicious little feast delivered here. I am tired of going to restaurants, and I must say that your place fascinates me. Everything is so well thought out, so perfectly designed."

"With pleasure. I'm very curious to know what happened. But give me a half hour to take a shower and change. I've had a hard day. Let's go up, shall we?"

I was surprised to see Rachel display such charm, and I must say it suited her better than professional dryness. I followed her up to the second floor.

"Will you show me around?"

"Of course. What would you like to drink? Champagne?"

I accepted with a smile.

"Are you coming from New York?"

"Yes, the investigation took longer than we thought."

I again admired the de Kooning. She opened the champagne bottle with style and sat down to pour. I proposed a toast.

"To our mutual success!"

She laughed, repeating the phrase with a hint of irony. The evening was promising.

"Are there two more floors?"

"Yes, a floor for each of life's activities. We can go upstairs if you'd like."

We left the books and the Klein blue. The next floor was devoted to the art of food. A large central kitchen opened up on two distinct spaces, one for big formal dinners, the other, more intimate, a glass-walled corner overlooking a garden. The color of that floor, a buttercup yellow, harmonized wonderfully with the ultramarine chairs. Just like on the first floor, a big canvas hung on the wall, dominated by red. The wide plank floorboards resembled the deck of a sailboat. A huge bouquet of peonies in a Mexican vase struck another note of color, pulling the whole look together.

"I built this house six years ago. Before that I lived in a converted garage in the suburbs."

"I love it. If I had a house, it's the style I would choose."

"Do you live in an apartment?"

"I don't live anywhere. No house, no apartment. I pick a different hotel every night."

"That's original."

"My life is rather complicated and I like change. My parents own a little house in Pensacola, as I told you. Maybe one day I'll have something built there. What color scheme is the top floor?"

"Come and see . . . It is the floor of rest, sleep."

The walls and the ceilings were painted the color of amaranth. The lighting was soft. There were a lot of books. We entered a large bedroom. I saw photos of Erwin, whose presence here was obsessive. A television system with retroprojection, second monitor, CDs, a bathroom in marble featuring veins the same shade as the walls. Two guest suites, each one just as well equipped for sleepless nights.

"Are you an insomniac?" I asked.

"Yes . . . I can only fall asleep in the morning . . . How did you guess?"

"I don't know, intuition."

"One's past comes back to visit at night."

"There is a way to free yourself from those things," I suggested.

"Don't mention psychotherapy to me."

"Are you against it?"

"Yes. I tried it for three years, but I was only able to reactivate the pain."

"There are other ways . . ."

"You'll have to tell me about them . . . Let me get ready . . . Wait for me on the second floor . . . There is an address book by the phone. Call Divine Cooking and mention my name. They are the best."

"Do you have any special request?"

"They make delicious whole fish. And I love chocolate."

"Me too."

"Don't order wine, I have an exceptional cellar."

"I hope you'll let me visit it . . ."

"It would be my pleasure for you to pick wine later . . ."

I went back downstairs. The evening was going to be full of surprises. She knew I knew certain things and probably thought I had missed the rest. I called Divine Cooking. They suggested a lobster salad, a turbot with sorrel, and a bitter chocolate cake. It sounded perfect. Out of curiosity, I leafed through Rachel's address book. Nordvensen's phone number wasn't listed. Sly. Maybe he would join us for dinner. A black magic dinner.

I looked at the CDs. There was a preponderance of jazz. I took out a recording by Archie Shepp and Dollar Brand and played it loud. The sound system was out of this world. I drank a little champagne and kicked back. Between recordings I thought. I supposed that Rachel, like all artists, had certain habits and that the *humfo* was probably located in the basement, with my soul and that of Mona. Like in Nordvensen's house.

Rachel appeared in a superb black dress of crushed velvet. Her fatigue seemed to have vanished. Her arms were bare and her hands, big, beautiful, and expressive, didn't wear any jewels.

"Were you listening to Archie Shepp?"

"I love music."

"Would you like to listen to something else?"

"No, I'd rather talk."

I poured some champagne for her. I noticed the makeup on her eyelids was tattooed. It hadn't changed in spite of the shower.

"So, tell me everything . . ."

"I'll start with Parker. He was manipulated by another man, who was probably in love with Erwin too. Actually, it seems, according to the present investigation, that Parker is innocent. He is a prominent voodoo specialist but, like many academicians, has never practiced what he teaches. In fact, letters from Erwin, *pots-têtes,* a large clay bowl, and a dagger had been placed in his apartment before I got there in order to incriminate him."

"What led you to the other man?"

"It wasn't hard. There are only three members of the Infinity Movement still alive. I started with the closest one, a man called Nordvensen who lives in an exquisite house in East Hampton."

"This name rings a bell . . . If you'll allow me . . ."

Rachel got up, booted up a Macintosh computer that was in the corner, scanned for a name.

"Yes, it's him . . . I designed that house in 1976. I can't believe this!"

"The house is magnificent. You never saw it?"

"Of course, I always supervise my jobs. I remember a tall, dry man with pale eyes, not very pleasant, but I had no idea he had known Erwin. What a strange coincidence."

"He must have known who you were because of Erwin, and maybe Erwin never mentioned his name because of the extraordinary evil power of that man."

"Do you really believe that?"

"I witnessed his power on a few people who practically died before my eyes."

The doorbell rang. Rachel pressed the intercom button and a stylish young man came up, carrying a large isothermal tray.

"Good evening, Ms. Zab, good evening, sir. I'll go

straight up. Would you like me to put the fish in the oven to keep it warm and finish its baking while you savor the appetizer?"

"Thank you, Peter. And then you may leave."

We went up with him. Rachel had set the little table. The dishes were Mexican, the glasses hand-blown. There was even a three-branch candelabra. After Peter had put the fish in the oven and served the salad, I paid him. One hundred and thirty-five dollars. I tipped him and suggested to Rachel that we go to the basement to select a bottle of wine.

The cellar was cool, kept at a constant temperature and humidity. Rachel showed me the Bordeaux, the Bourgogne, the Loire Valley wines, the Italian wines, the Spanish and Portuguese wines, and finally the California wines. There must have been four or five thousand bottles.

"I prefer the Bordeaux. I only drink red," she explained, "do you mind? Of course, I have excellent white ones as well."

"I defer to you."

"How about a Mouton-Rothschild '82?"

"Wonderful."

As we emerged from the cellar, I noticed three additional doors.

"Does this lead to the garage?"

"Yes. Are you interested in cars?"

"I am interested in everything."

She pushed the door open, turned on the light. There was a night blue convertible Lotus.

"Not bad. Nice toy. And what about the other doors over there?"

"Please, don't ask me to show you my washer/dryer, not to mention the rest of the junk I keep in that room . . . Let's go back upstairs. We don't want the fish to be overcooked."

I noticed that the laundry room was sealed by a steel-plated door with a triple lock, rather unusual for a utility room, but I followed her politely. There would be time to go back down later, after dessert.

We started with the lobster and truffle salad, deliciously seasoned. Rachel uncorked the bottle with an expert's ease, sniffed the cork, poured the wine, twirled it gently in her glass, smelled it, tasted it, and served me.

"Superb vintage."

I thought the wine a bit cool. She read my mind.

"People think *chambré* means at the present temperature of the room, but it's a mistake. The temperature must be that of a room before houses were heated, a little under sixty degrees."

Rachel went to get the fish. I followed her, taking the salad plates back to the kitchen. The turbot came with a white butter sauce and garden vegetables.

"So, go on, tell me what happened at Nordvensen's."

"Well, he tried to kill me."

"Kill you!?"

"Yes . . ."

"How?"

"By voodoo . . . It was fascinating . . . I caught him doing obscure incantations in front of a clay bowl. He was concentrating so hard he didn't see me walk in. And then the most amazing thing happened . . ."

"Do tell . . ."

"There was water in the bowl and my image appeared."

"It must have been a reflection."

"No, it wasn't the right angle."

"And then?"

"He lifted a dagger and was about to stab the image when he was shot in the mouth. The bullet came out through the cerebellum."

"Who shot him?"

"Probably a protective spirit."

"You're kidding! This sounds like science fiction . . ."

"Yes, you're right, because then I fell asleep and Nord-vensen somehow disappeared and hasn't been seen since."

"Do you take hallucinogenics?"

"My generation doesn't take that stuff."

"You're putting me on, then . . ."

"Not at all. This morning I even received a rather un-pleasant letter from him . . ."

"From whom?"

"Nordvensen . . . The letter warned me he was going to kill me slowly, as well as my girlfriend, Princess Bashma's sister. By the way, do you like rap?"

"I love it . . ."

"Would you allow me to offer you Bashma's new album? She had just recorded it before being killed by voodoo. There is a song about Erwin on it, strangely enough."

"What?"

She was more than a little surprised by that. I pressed my advantage.

"Yes, the producers had decided to remove it from the album, but I convinced them to keep it as an homage to your brother. Also, it's a fresh subject, it's never been done in a rap song. There was a mix-up about stolen master tapes, but it turned out to be just p.r. because the master tapes were al-ready being pressed. They used the publicity to warm up the audience."

This improvised piece of news didn't provoke any reac-tion in her. She was beginning to show signs of instability and I was soon going to go for the kill, but before that, I wanted a taste of the bitter chocolate cake and to finish the bottle of Mouton-Rothschild.

"Tell me about Erwin . . . I have great empathy for him . . ."

Rachel remained quiet for a moment.

"As I told you last time, we were very close. Our parents were traditional Jews and they did not take well to Erwin's wish to be an actor. I was the only one to support his rebellion. When he turned eighteen, he left home and I think that's when he became homosexual."

"It's also a form of rebellion."

"We wrote to each other every day and kept the fires stoked. I wanted to become a painter. I was rather gifted. A well-known artist to whom I had had the courage to show my drawings even went to talk to my parents, but to no avail. That's the primary reason I chose to become an architect later on."

"Did you have a good shrink?"

"One of the best."

"Did you tell him you slept with Erwin, Princess?"

I thought she was going to throw up on the table. She became hysterical and insulted me. She threw the wine bottle at my head but missed me. She fell to the ground, seized by violent convulsions. I picked her up in my arms, carried her upstairs, and put her, still dressed, under a cold shower. Eventually she calmed down enough to catch her breath. I pulled her out and threw her roughly on the bed. I sat down beside her and caressed her throat.

"You know, Princess, it's good to talk, it helps to sleep . . ."

"Bastard," she snarled.

"Let me tell you how it happened . . . One day, Erwin and you were invited by Nord to take a beautiful trip and you met a real voodoo priest . . . Papa Mosso . . ."

Princess was shaking all over. Her eyes projected an intense hate.

"Nord had no talent but here was this young girl, full of

hate and rage, who had the gift . . . Papa Mosso, being the most accomplished of voodoo priests, recognized a true talent and made her his disciple. You fell in love with your new power, became his wife and his favorite disciple and, like me, he knew you had slept with your brother. Princess is a lovely name but you don't really deserve it, do you? Thanks to Nord's money—among other things he bought you art, didn't he?—you quickly became successful and once you didn't need him anymore you manipulated him because something unpleasant had happened: you found out that a certain Kate Henning had had the bad judgment to take her name back. You had killed her father and mother in revenge for your brother, but you also wanted the daughter. You learnt that Bashma had hidden Kate's father's papers. She thought she was singing about the horrible commie 'witch'-hunt, but the real witch was you."

Princess tried to get up, but my hand on her larynx stopped her. Her strength was coming back.

"Zulu, you will die like all the others . . . You've got to understand that . . ."

"No . . ."

"So kill me, but somehow I think two cases of self-defense might be a bit too much, even for a cop."

"You don't get it . . . I accept your magic fight . . ."

Princess laughed diabolically.

"Okay, Zulu . . . You're brave . . . Wonderful, Zulu!"

"We are going to go down to your *humfo*."

"Never!"

I threw her across the room. She understood that the next time she would go straight through the window. She got up, found the keys, and we went downstairs.

12

P rincess's worried eyes were darting around looking for a way out. She looked as if she would have loved to stab me with a kitchen knife. I roughed her up a little. I couldn't wait to go to hell. She was shaky when she opened the locks. It wasn't so much the fear, more the excitement, knowing that if, indeed, I accepted the magic fight, she was sure to win. An oil lamp was burning on the altar.

The *humfo* looked like Nordvensen's, the central post made of wood, the machete, the red tunic. There were pants folded on a mattress. She closed the door, lit the candles in front of the images of the gods and a big black-and-white picture of Papa Mosso. There were cigars, bottles, candle holders, oil lamps, cups, bowls, *pots-têtes*. The ritual dagger was hanging from the center post next to a magic stick. There was a chair made of woven wicker, and behind it shelves on which were displayed clay bowls and paper bags containing hair, nail clippings, rings, pieces of fabric, and the pictures of her victims. Princess was well organized, everything classified and filed in alphabetical order, so I had no trouble finding my file and those of Mona, Kate, and Bashma. I was surprised by the sheer number of files. There were thirty-six of them.

Moving like a cheetah, Princess grabbed the dagger and tried to hit me with it, but my left foot caught her smack in the stomach and she collapsed on the earthen floor.

I couldn't see any live animals, but there was an unpleasant odor in the *humfo*. Following my nose, I went to the altar. A covered clay bowl, about the size of a salad tureen, contained a human liver in the process of mummification. It wasn't quite desiccated yet.

"Hi, Nord," I said casually.

Princess got to her feet, sat on her throne, caught her breath.

"You came for Nord after I killed him," I told her. "You had even thought to have him write me a letter before I came."

"I am a lot smarter than you think, Zulu," she said, suddenly very composed.

"How do you achieve that beautiful serenity, Princess?"

"The gods and the forces are with me. You should never have walked into this sacred place, because you are now in my power."

"I saw your files, Princess. They are overcrowded."

"Thirty-four people have died. The only ones left are you, Zulu, and Mona."

"Who were the others? Were you practicing on them?"

"The men who took Erwin away from me, and a few others who stood in the way of my career."

"It must be fun to kill people like that . . . Always with the dagger?"

"There are other ways."

Princess had the air of an eminent university professor giving an interview. With the number of victims, all the documents found in the room, I could have tried to have her indicted for murder, but I knew what would happen. After a few years in a straitjacket, Princess would magically return to her present activities.

I looked into Bashma's file and wasn't surprised to find the master tapes wrapped in newspaper.

"How do you manage to hire the kids who spray-paint the walls?" I asked.

"They are street scum, gay hustlers. I am their goddess. They would kill for me. I support them."

"I see. A program of social rehabilitation, right, Princess?"

"How did you come to suspect me?"

I laughed, looked in her eyes that were eerily shiny.

"Zulu's system. We each have our own magic."

"Do you really accept the magic fight?"

"It's more fun than slashing your neck with a machete, don't you think? It's time for you to realize that you can't go on killing everyone on the whole planet."

"No, Zulu and Mona will be enough."

"It's too bad. You are a good architect. All this insanity is the result of puritanism, yours and Henning's. I have a certain sympathy for Erwin. He was the first victim, the only one who didn't get perverted by this lineage of crazy witches. I am going to take the little bags of hair and nails, your pictures, Mona's soul and mine. These clay salad bowls are very pretty. I suppose you've got clay and a potter's wheel in your garage. When women turn fifty, they often become interested in craft. It makes them feel good to connect with matter, create something with their hands."

"Take everything you want, Zulu."

"You must look great in costume . . . I also want the red shirt and the pants."

I saw her bristle.

"Maybe also the magic stick and the dagger."

I made a pile of all these objects by the door. Princess was watching me with crazy eyes.

"I am going to leave you, Princess. I declare magic war on you."

"You give too much importance to these objects. The supreme art I learned from Papa Mosso doesn't require ritual. Only the pure power of the spirit matters."

"Ciao, Princess, welcome to hell."

She moved her lips, bared her teeth, and blew like an enraged hyena.

"Oh, I was forgetting . . ."

I came close to her, produced a pair of scissors that I had lifted from the kitchen. She understood I was going to cut her fingernails and hair. I was expecting some kind of violent reaction, but with a horrible laugh, she let me do it.

"You will suffer a lot, Zulu, and all the people who will try to protect you will know the same death as you. You will see, it's worse than hell. It will start in a few hours."

I tied her up with a length of rope in such a way that she could free herself after a few hours of struggle. Before I left, I took the cigar from the altar. It was a Monte Cristo. I lit it up at the flame of the oil lamp, glanced at Princess one last time, and carried my gear upstairs.

I found a big tote bag in the kitchen and packed all my treasures in it. I made sure there were still available seats on the last flight to Miami, made a reservation, and called a cab. As I closed the door behind me, I heard the crazy Princess yelling magic incantations.

Atlanta airport. While I was walking through the metal detector, a friendly looking black woman, seeing all my junk, asked me:

"How was the weather in Mexico?"

"It's a magic country. I hope the X rays won't destroy the magic."

"Don't worry . . . You'll be able to put all that on your fireplace mantel."

The first-class cabin was quiet. I drank a Perrier with a twist, had a quick nap, then called Live Crew to come pick me up at the airport.

I began to observe myself minutely, becoming acutely aware of each and every nuance inside my body, waiting for the illness to strike. I made an effort to get rid of the thought that Princess could act on me. I told myself that a bullet was quick and sure. What was bothering me was to take part in a fight in which I was impotent.

It made me feel better to see Live Crew. Lita and Roy looked terrific.

"Still alive," Roy noticed.

"I am under serious voodoo threat."

"You better be. Do you realize you interrupted a major stage in my education?"

"He is making a lot of progress," Lita said. "Very talented guy."

"Did you buy the tickets for Kingston?"

"Your flight leaves at nine thirty-two tomorrow morning. We've just put Clementine to bed. Boy, is she carrying on! She loves to party."

"Did you buy Mayan salad bowls in Atlanta?" asked Roy.

"Yep. One of them even had a human liver in it."

"Oh, gross!" Lita said.

"Where do you want me to drop you off?" I asked.

"We're not in such a rush," Lita said. "We can take you to the Fruit Market, wait until you finish dealing with Sweetie Pie Speed, take you back to your love nest with your little meteorite, and come get you tomorrow morning. No sweat."

"No, I have other plans."

"Okay, boss!" screamed my two foot soldiers in unison. We jumped into the car and hit the highway.

"We had the car washed."

"And tuned up."

"And the tire pressure checked."

"Well done, kiddos."

Lita helped me off with my jacket, strapped on my holster with its cold black peacemaker in it, lifted my white pants, fastened a knife underneath.

"Do you remember the kid who spray-painted the wall?"

"Yeah."

"Well, he is right behind us, with five buddies."

"All right, finally, some action! This case was turning into geriatric care," Lita said.

Roy, who was sitting on the backseat, his cap in the wind, swiveled around.

"It's a souped-up Chevy. They might be loaded."

"They want the salad bowls, possibly our livers as well."

"I refuse to die for a salad bowl," Roy said. "Go ahead, show 'em what you got . . ."

"Fuck! There's a biker with them."

"Let's take care of the Chevy first."

I pushed the engine a bit, but they stayed on my tail. I

had to find another way. Souped-up cars always have a problem with their shock absorbers. I knew some rotten roads; the worst ones in the whole state of Florida. At the exit to Paradise City, I was going to put them through a series of tight hairpin turns. The rodeo started. The bike handled it better than the low rider. We had a few near misses. The Chevy skidded left and right. The BMW's engine screamed. The gears shifted in a fraction of a second. At each curve, Live Crew gave me an exact report on the situation.

"A couple more curves like that and they're gone."

That's what happened. I heard the sound of crunching metal.

"What about the biker?"

"We could shoot him," Lita suggested.

"They've just poured fresh sand on Madagascar Avenue," Roy offered.

I went in that direction, stomped the gas pedal to hit the intersection with maximum power. I slammed the brakes and skidded but managed to control the wheel. The biker, after an improbable arc, crashed through the window of a bodega.

I cruised slowly into the Fruit Market. It didn't take me long to notice the Chevy. They knew my habits. The car was parked under a tree, all lights off. They were making a bad mistake. I had a card up my sleeve.

I picked up Mona. She realized that something was wrong; Speed smelled it too. I parked behind his car and jumped in with the dough.

"All the money is here. There's a problem, though."

"The yellow Chevy?"

"Yeah, these kids have been following me since I picked up the cash."

Sweetie Pie Speed flashed a mean smile.

"Now that I got it, it's my problem. They can't be driving into the protected zone and get away with it."

Speed signaled with his headlights. There was strange movement: the hookers disappeared as if by magic. The two cross streets were suddenly blocked by vehicles and the yellow Chevy was surrounded by a dozen pimps. The kids must have been scared shitless, what with the sawed-off shotgun barrels, the Uzis, all the artillery aimed at their faces. They were forced out of their car, and in seven or eight seconds the block was back to normal, as if nothing had happened. Only the johns had remained on the sidewalks, like scarecrows.

"How would you like them, sliced or cubed?" Speed asked.

"I need them refrigerated for three days."

"You got it. Consider it a present."

Speed counted his dough, got out of his ride, slapped me on the back, and came up to Mona.

"Bye, girl."

"Bye, Sweetie Pie Speed."

"I am sad, Mona. You're leaving the Fruit Market. You're the best whore I ever had."

Mona got out of the car, kissed Speed.

"We've had a good time together," she said, slipping her night's cut into his hand.

Speed turned to me.

"Zulu, the day you want to get rid of her, I'll buy her back from you. If you need a couple of hot little numbers, I can train them for you. We can get into business together. I am the best. I should open a school. I am to whores what West Point is to the army."

"Thanks, Speed, take it slow."

"Take it slow, General!" Live Crew screamed. They hadn't missed our exchange.

"No respect for their elders, but they have a sense of humor," commented Speed, lighting up a joint as fat as a billy club. He watched us leave with nostalgia. We drove out of the Fruit Market while Mona yelled and jumped for joy, hugging my neck.

"It might be dangerous to sleep at your place," I told Mona. "Let's get a room near the airport."

"With surveillance parking?" asked Roy.

"Yep."

"In that case, maybe we could get two rooms."

"Okay, Live Crew, I can't deny you anything."

"Don't get them next to each other, Zulu. We would keep you two up all night."

I closed the bedroom door. A feeling of extraordinary peace filled me. Mona was drunk on freedom.

Sitting on the edge of the bed, she chanted, rythmically rocking back and forth:

I can't believe it . . .
I can't believe it . . .
I can't believe it . . .
I can't believe it . . .
I can't believe it . . .
I can't believe it . . .
I can't believe it . . .
I can't believe it . . .
I can't believe it . . .
I can't believe it . . .
I can't believe it . . .
I can't believe it . . .
I can't believe it . . .

I can't believe it . . .
I can't believe it . . .

I let her go on. Some movements shouldn't be interrupted. I called Mono.

"What motherfucker is calling me at three o'clock in the
morning? . . . Yeah . . . It can only be . . ."

"Zulu . . ."

"That's what I thought . . . It better be worth it if you
want to keep your balls, pal . . ."

Mona was still going, louder and louder:

I can't believe it . . .
I believe can't it . . .
I it believe can't . . .
Believe can't I it . . .
Can't believe it I . . .

"Who's that rapper? Def stuff. Very cool . . ."

"Not bad, huh? . . ."

"You're weird, Zulu."

"Nobody ever said otherwise . . ."

"I've been auditioning for three solid days trying to find
rap's next queen, and you call me up at three o'clock in the
morning with a voice that has the beat, dripping with soul
. . . What's her name?"

"Ha! Ha!"

"I'm coming. If she's got the face and the ass to go with
the voice, a hundred percent wild, I sign her."

"You've got flair, Mono, I can't deny that."

"I believe in magic, in surprises . . . in what's fresh and
down . . . I've never heard a rapper that grabs you by the balls
like that one. Where are you?"

"Sheraton Hotel, room 2008."

"Don't move. I'll be right over."

"Do you remember, when I came to see you, you asked who paid me?"

"Sure . . ."

"Surprise! I've been working for you the last five days."

"What are you talking about?"

"Since I risked my life, and continue to do so, it has been costing you three thousand dollars per day, plus five thousand for expenses . . . A discount for you, my friend . . ."

"You're un-fucking-believable, Zulu! Do you think I am going to fork over that much green for an unknown rapper! Do you realize how much it costs to launch new product?"

"I don't want to hear that word. What I am delivering is super fresh, man, very live."

"Maybe, but it's not worth more than three thousand commission."

"I am going to hang up—"

"Just a minute, Zulu . . . What about—"

"The tapes? Boy, are you slow . . . Actually, I've got them right here . . ."

"Holy cow, great! Jeesus, do you really?"

"Yep, both of them, U-matic Sony tapes with the Rapadise Records label. Do you still find the price too high?"

"You are a genius, Zulu. A genius. By the way, how old is the kid?"

"Young, man, real young."

"Deal. Can you give me credit until the banks open, for the dough?"

"Yo."

"I'll be there in fifteen minutes. I'll bring champagne."

I hung up, looked at Mona. She was gone, way out there. Her face shone with an inner glow that no one would ever be able to put out. She was still running her long-playing rap.

While I waited for Mono, I put Mona's clay bowl and mine in the bathtub and called the bar.

"I'm thirsty."

"What would you like, sir?"

"Do you have big bottles of Perrier?"

"Yes, sir."

"Good. Bring me about a hundred of them."

The bartender laughed.

"I'm serious, man. A hundred."

"Very well, sir. It'll be five hundred dollars."

"The same as two bottles of Dom Perignon."

"Exactly."

"Hurry up. I'll give you fifty dollars to open them."

The bartender showed up five minutes later, the bottles in twelve-packs, crowded on a hand truck. Eurydice had mentioned spring water, and with Perrier, I couldn't go wrong, it was written on the bottle. Okay, it was carbonated, but it was spring water, so even the bubbles were natural. The label said so.

The bartender peeked discreetly at Mona, like a guy who brings breakfast to a naked woman. And Mona *was* naked, body and soul.

The bartender was opening, pouring, opening, pouring, opening, pouring. It's not a rap. I'll stop right here. Repetitive poetry has its limits.

"It's the most fun thing I've done in about a week," the barman said.

"What was the last one?"

"Evian water for a nut who was traveling with a huge goldfish called Pharaoh."

"How many bottles?"

"Thirty. The fish had a swimming pool at home."

"Pharaoh . . ."

"Oh look . . . your salad bowls are melting . . ."

"That's the point."

"Don't you like salad?"

"No."

Mono arrived with a portable tape recorder. He set up a mike, sat down in a chair, fascinated. I placed the master tapes on his lap. He didn't even open the boxes. Now Mona was screaming, but she was still chilling. She stopped an hour later, dripping with sweat. She peeled her dress and caught her breath, naked on the white sheet. Two minutes later, Mono came back to earth.

"Man, it was great, great. We're going to get two hits back to back."

"I forgot to tell you there is a condition to our deal."

"Yeah, what?"

"I want you to include the song about McCarthyism on Bashma's album."

"Why?"

"Because she died for that and this girl right here will tell the rest of the story."

"Great idea."

"I even have a title for her first album . . ."

"Yeah?"

"*Back from Hell . . .*"

"It's good. I like it. It'll sell . . . I'll put her together with the best backup musicians. She'll have to do some work for a few months, but by the time *Pure Steel* hits the charts, I'll launch her . . . By the way, what's her name?"

"Pussy Queen," Mona said, laughing.

She got up, stood on the bed, assumed a sculptural pose, and said:

"I want to be photographed like this for the album cover."

"It's fucking beautiful," Mono marveled, "but it won't be approved."

"So what, we'll reprint the cover with a little white square stamped 'Censored.' "

"I love you, 'Pussy Queen.' Not only do you have rage in your belly, but you've got great fucking marketing ideas."

"The sky's the limit, Mono."

"Stop by at my office tomorrow to sign the contracts. Do you need cash?"

"I haven't got a penny," Mona lied.

"I'll give you ten thousand dollars in advance."

"For that kind of money, you get my left foot."

Mono laughed.

"Plus, she's got brains . . . Okay, we'll negotiate."

"We're leaving for Kingston in the morning," she said.

"Then I'll expect you when you come back. Meanwhile, what do I tell the press about the master tapes?"

"Keep everything quiet until we get back and then I'll tell you everything. There's enough for a dozen magazine features, believe me."

"I believe you, Zulu. You know, if one day you're thinking of getting into a different line of work, let me know, I'll hire you as my music director. You understand rap and you bring me the gold nuggets."

"Don't forget what you owe me."

"As soon as you come back . . . I'll get a great photographer, we'll have a session, 'Pussy Queen.' "

Mono kissed his new star. He was foaming at the mouth

with pleasure. He slapped me on the back again, still icy and hard.

"You should do some Chinese stretching exercises, Mono. Your hands are a bit stiff."

Mono laughed, took off his right white glove. He had an aluminum paw.

"Nam . . ." he said, walking away.

Mona jumped into my arms, her legs around my waist.

"I think I can knock 'em dead."

"You are going to be a big hit."

"It's great to go to Kingston."

"It's going to be hard."

"Why?"

"We're going to fight death."

I went to the bathroom, Mona still hanging from me. The clay bowls were completely dissolved, collapsed upon one another in the Perrier bubbles.

"Do you take clay baths for your rheumatism, Zulu?"

"No, but you know, in some hotels, the bathrooms are just not very clean."

I stirred the bath with my hand and opened the drain. I rinsed the tub and Mona and I took a shower. Then I jammed the door shut, kept my gun close to me, and called Brad. He was used to being woken up and had developed the art of sounding alert at all times.

"Hi, it's Zulu."

"I was worried about you in my sleep."

"I have very important documents in my hotel room. I am at the Sheraton Hotel, room 2008."

"Anything new?"

"You bet. Rachel Zab is the one."

"No kidding?"

"I want you to take the first plane to Atlanta. Take a video team with you. It will be something unique in the police archives. You are about to record a voodoo fight to the death live."

"How do I get into her place?"

"I have the keys. She will be in such a state that even if you bring a whole TV crew with you, she won't even realize it. You'll have to be careful the first three days. You'll see her make some pottery and after a night in the moonlight, the two clay bowls she needs for our execution will be ready."

"I'll bring my best men. I'm on my way. Give me an hour."

"We'll just have the time to grab a little sleep."

Mona smiled at me, lay down on the white sheet, slowly opened her legs, and murmured:

"Come and suck my candy, Zulu."

I couldn't resist. When Brad knocked at the door, my mouth and whole face were still shiny with Mona's pleasure. Brad came in alone. He examined the photos, the envelopes, noticed that each clay bowl was scarred with the impact of the ritual dagger. Mona pretended to sleep.

"Are you sure you can make it?"

"I hope so, but let me tell you something. Don't make the same mistake I did. Don't kill her. It is the first and last time such a battle will be on film; it is very important for the world to see, and we'll be able to use it to nail all the mouths of all the rationalists shut."

"Okay, I won't interfere. But are you sure you are well protected?"

"I think so."

"You are a character."

Brad hugged me. I drew a plan of Princess's house for him, and he took the map with him.

I ordered breakfast for eight o'clock, retook my position between Mona's legs, placed my hands under her buttocks and my head on her stomach while she stroked my head. The movements slowed down, I felt two little contractions under my right hand, her breathing deepened, and we fell asleep.

13

There was no time for the really long kiss I wanted to give
Mona. We had to pick up Eurydice and the plane was leaving
at nine-thirty. Mona jumped out of the car to buy herself a pink
cotton dress, as if she were going away on vacation. Eurydice
was waiting on her doorstep, wearing a white dress, a straw hat,
and carrying a little suitcase. But we were not going for a dream
week on the beach among coconut trees.

Eurydice was very serious and focused. Mona remained
silent. The plane was flying toward Kingston. I told Eurydice
about my evening with Princess and that I had brought back her
red tunic, hair, and nail clippings. Eurydice nodded, then closed
her eyes and withdrew into herself. She was either praying or
repeating magic formulas, for her lips were moving.

I refused all drinks and food for Eurydice. Mona had an orange juice, I had a Perrier. Mona pressed herself against me. She was getting scared.

A little before we landed, Eurydice opened her eyes and smiled at us kindly. I called the stewardess, who brought her a glass of water.

"Did you dissolve the clay bowls in spring water, as I told you to do?"

"Yes. I even brought back the bags with our nail and hair clippings."

"There are other ways, but they are less efficient. You can write the name of the victim on a piece of paper and mix it with the clay. We have three days to get ready in Mr. Clesh's *humfo*. You must follow my instructions exactly. Your lives depend on that. During these three days you will have to purify yourselves and prepare for the battle that will follow. I want you to empty yourselves. You will be initiated, I will receive you as my disciples, and from then on we will be completely bound together. During that time you will abstain from all sexual relations. Any mistake, any lapse in concentration, might be fatal."

Eurydice was speaking in gentle tones, but an extraordinary authority emanated from her. She was becoming another woman, the woman she had been in the past, at her father's side, adored, powerful.

Princess unties herself. She moves like a somnambulist. Her face looks like that of a mummy, filled with hate, and fear of the unknown. She breathes strangely, utters little cries like those of an infant or an animal. When she gets back to the first floor, it is daylight. She calls her assistant, tells her dryly that she is closing her office for a week. She goes to the kitchen, drinks half a bottle of rum before going to her bedroom. She opens a closet, rummages around, tossing dresses and suits about the room. She hollers and moans.

Finally she finds a red shirt, gets undressed, puts on a pair of black pants. She goes to Erwin's framed photo, breaks the glass against a corner of the dresser, tears out the print, puts it on the bed and lies on it, uttering long mourning moans.

We took a cab. Eurydice asked the driver to stop in order to buy cigars, candles, rum, white clothes for Mona and me before navigating the road to Black River. I had chosen a fairly new and comfortable car. The trip took us less than four hours. I sent the cab back, and as we were approaching the small houses that seemed buried in the jungle, Clesh came out. His clothes were white and freshly laundered. He came to Eurydice. They held hands and twirled around, performing a kind of minuet, rolling their heads against each other, exchanging long ritual salutations.

Clesh greeted Mona and me. His wife and his daughter took care of us while Clesh and Eurydice disappeared into the *humfo* to salute the gods and set their strategy.

Princess drains the bottle of rum while rummaging around in her files for a photo of me and one of Mona. She looks at the pictures with cruelty. She goes back to the basement, opens a room adjacent to the garage. A barrel full of clay, a potter's wheel, water. She places a first lump of clay on the wheel and rips Mona's photo in tiny pieces that she incorporates into the clay. Princess operates the wheel with her foot. With her wet hands, she sculpts the first bowl into its characteristic shape. She does the same with my photo, makes the other bowl, then washes her hands. She opens the garage door, checks on the sky that is devoid of clouds. She carries the clay bowls upstairs and exposes them to the sun on a terrace with southern exposure. In her bedroom, in a drawer full of underwear, she finds a ritual dagger similar to the others. She swallows two sleeping pills and lies down on Erwin's picture. The phone rings. She doesn't wake up.

Mona was taken to one hut, I into another. We were given a pitcher and a glass. We could hear Clesh's and Eurydice's alternating incantations. Polynice was taking care of Mona, Mrs. Clesh of me.

"Wait in peace for the Father and the Mother of the Gods to give you their instructions."

I found myself alone, overwhelmed by the sudden, naked silence.

Sometime later, Eurydice and Clesh came to get us. They took us through the woods to a spring from which the water flowed into a natural basin. They told us to take off our clothes and to get into the cool water, which was as high as my waist. Eurydice and Clesh got into the water and rubbed us hard, one after the other, reciting different ritual chants. Each had a personal style. Clesh cupped water into his palms and let it flow over our heads and down all over our bodies. Eurydice was sprinkling us more violently and sometimes hollering. We left our clothes by the spring and walked back to the *humfo* wrapped in strips of white cotton.

In the *humfo*, Eurydice asked us to kiss the ground three times in front of the altar. Then they drew circles around us and washed us with *trempé*. At times one or the other screamed, took a machete and whipped it through space. Eurydice hit us a few times with a stick she had picked up in the forest. She also hit us with her hand in various places, addressing the gods in Creole. Sometimes she walked away to the altar, drank some rum, and came back to us looking like an angry warrior. Polynice brought our white clothes.

Mona was the first to start shaking, and to speak in an unintelligible tongue. Her body shook with spasms. Then it was my turn. Eurydice and Clesh watched us carefully. I saw that sometimes they seemed to take something from Mona's body and toss it into space. I soon lost consciousness of my surroundings, my whole body shaking with violent spasms.

I woke up in my hut. Eurydice was there, reassuring.

"The protecting gods came to observe you. In three days they will come down into you. You will each stay alone in your hut, in silence. Clesh and I will come every day to take you to a warm bath. Then we will cover your bodies with a powerful oil. You will eat what we will bring you and sleep on your right-hand side, on a mat, on the floor."

Eurydice washed my hair with a concoction of plants that had a strong and unpleasant smell. From a clay pot she cupped a brownish mixture made of blood, wine, grilled corn, rice, bread, and caramelized sugar. She spread this mixture on mombin leaves that she folded and spread on my skull, my forehead, and my closed eyelids, keeping them in place with white cotton bandages.

"You must not take this off."

Eurydice left me after a short incantation. I lay down on the mat and fell asleep on my side.

Princess wakes up in the middle of the night. She drinks more rum and checks out the clay bowls. She covers them to protect them from the humidity of the night. Then she goes down to the *humfo,* lights fresh candles. She covers her forehead and her arms with a kind of grease she scrapes from a clay pot. She lights a cigar and performs a jumpy dance around the center-post, blowing smoke toward the sky. She yells incantations and stops when the cigar butt burns her fingers. Out of breath, she collapses on the ground, shaken up by convulsions as though demons had taken possession of her body.

I woke up, surprised not to see any daylight. I felt a presence and almost immediately heard Eurydice's voice.

"Good, my son. You have rested. Now I will rub your body with oil and you will remain seated, your back against the door, until I come back."

I heard her walk away. A few quiet hours passed by, interrupted by intense anxieties.

When Eurydice came back, she was carrying a plate of white rice and a broiled chicken neck that she told me to chew and swallow completely, bones and all. There was a tall glass of water. She waited until I had finished eating and drinking, then she took away the tray without a word.

I listened to the jungle from my seat, the filtered sounds coming from the *humfo* where Clesh and Eurydice spoke with the gods. Their voices were alternately soft, violent, loving, and terrifying, and it seemed to me I heard the sounds of a machete slashing through space. I also heard the screams of a sacrificed rooster, the beating of his wings while he flew without his head.

Several drummers came. At the end of the day, one of them played longer than the others, and I understood, from their conversation, that Eurydice had hired him.

Toward evening, Clesh came to wash me in warm water but didn't remove the mask that blinded me. The ingredients were beginning to ferment with the heat, and the stench they gave off was almost unbearable. The fermentation, though, produced a warmth that was somewhat reassuring.

Princess gets up, she bows three times in front of the altar, kisses the picture of Papa Mosso, then addresses him in a long prayer in Creole. She drinks rum, smokes another cigar, lights up more candles, and lifts the plate that covers the clay pot containing Nordvensen's liver. She talks to it in Creole, brutal, choppy sounds. She gives it orders then blows on it three times before replacing the plate. Princess lies down in front of the altar, on the earthen floor, her arms akimbo. She mutters the same incantation over and over.

She gets up and rubs the ritual dagger with the same grease with which she had rubbed her body. She places the dagger in front of Papa Mosso and begs him to give the weapon magic powers. It is the first time she uses English.

Eurydice came to see me. She touched my hands, my heart, and my feet with an armful of leaves. I ate a banana and some grilled corn, then she left me alone in the night full of terrifying images. I heard Mona scream. Steps. She slowly calmed down.

I fell into sleep, dreaming that my body was erupting into fireworks. Luminous projections radiated from me and streamed into the surrounding space.

The next day followed the same pattern, but a feeling of lightness progressively took me over. It was my turn to scream into the night. Maybe Mona was blacker than me, closer to the gods and their mysterious forces. Eurydice came to see me; she took my hands in hers and only told me to let the images come out of my soul without fear, for the images are only projections of my own anxiety, they had no substance. I finally calmed down and the last day went on like the previous ones, with less fear in both me and Mona, for I didn't hear her scream anymore.

Wrapped in a blanket, hallucinating, Princess is watching the moon rise and gradually lights the dry clay bowls, throwing a vaporous shadow on the wooden table. She has twelve cigars, a matchbox, and a bottle of rum to measure the time. She drinks, lights up the first cigar. You can barely see her face in the moonlight. When she has finished smoking three cigars, she turns the clay bowls around quarter by quarter to expose every angle to the moonbeams. Time passes, marked by the red embers and the terrible words chanted in the night.

At midnight we were led by the hand to the *humfo*. The drums started to beat, Eurydice removed the bandages, scrubbed our skulls thoroughly with brewed herbs until the smell of fermentation was washed away. She purified our bodies one more time, ordered us to bow in front of Clesh, in front of her, and in front of the altar. Polynice and Clesh's wife attended the ceremony. They clapped their hands. The drummer, letting himself go, played for the gods. Clesh and Eurydice drank and smoked the cigar. Suddenly, Mona's body started to shake, she tried to move, the beat of the drums abruptly changed to the rhythm of a possessed dance. Eurydice addressed the gods by their names, begged them to come down, to accept the offerings displayed on the altar. A long spasm ran through me; suddenly I became entranced. The drum skins exploded inside of me and I tore through the thin partition that separates the rational world from that of the spirits. A scream came out of my mouth, and I forgot myself completely.

Princess finishes the last cigar and drains the bottle of rum. She carries the bowls, one after the other, into the *humfo.*

She loses her footing a couple of times and catches herself at the last minute to keep the bowls from shattering. She bows, kisses the ground three times, then kisses the picture of Papa Mosso.

Hollering, she picks up Nordvensen's liver, hurls it to the ground between the altar and the centerpost. Her calls are now strident screams. She sits down, places the bowls in front of her, clutches the ritual dagger.

It was still night. I came to, feeling Eurydice's fresh breath on my eyes.

"Wake up, son, wake to the light . . ."

Mona had already come out of her trance. The drum slowed in cadence. Eurydice and Clesh gave us candles that they had lit. We walked out of the *humfo.*

"You are going to face death, but I will protect you with all my powers. Do not ever lose faith!"

Clesh led the way, holding the machete. Then came Mona, followed by me and Eurydice, who held in her hand Princess's red tunic. We walked deep into the jungle.

Princess pours water into each of the clay bowls. She runs her hands over them, concentrating. Her whole body is sweating and shaky. Suddenly, an image appears in the first bowl; it is Mona. Princess goes to the second bowl, performs the same gestures until my body appears.

She manages to keep both images simultaneously with screams, incantations, demonic mutterings.

She jumps up, picks up the liver, cuts it in pieces, throws them one by one in the bowls.

It felt as though my entrails were being ripped out of my belly and I threw myself to the ground, screaming with pain, at the same time as Mona. The machete whirled to the four cardinal points to slash the evil spell while Eurydice extracted the illness with her hands and threw it to the night, until we were able to get up and continue our walk ever deeper into the forest. We arrived at a cemetery in which white crosses were gleaming in the moonlight. Eurydice took our hands and said:

"Do not be afraid of this dead man. Only he can save you."

Shaking under the moonlight we were subjected to additional attacks, which Eurydice repelled using the same violence while Clesh was digging the ground with his machete.

Princess looks at the pieces of liver falling though us. Then, when the images are peaceful once again, with the point of her ritual dagger she strikes the images, slashing them furiously. The water turns pink.

Mona and I felt our skins opening to the blade. Mona's screams were louder than mine. Eurydice shoved us to the ground. Clesh slashed through space. Mona and I, pressed against each other, felt the body of Eurydice covering us. The pain disappeared immediately. Eurydice kept chanting her incantations without suffering any obvious pain. Her burning body protected us.

Princess utters a cry, then another. She tears her tunic off her body; huge cuts open her flesh; the blood beads at the same time that the water in the bowls becomes purified. The evil spells turn against her, tear her apart. Princess runs to the altar, grabs Papa Mosso's photo, jerks it out of its frame, rolls it and beats the surface of the water with it.

We felt the beating as powerfully as if we had been hit with baseball bats. Eurydice too screamed with pain, then stumbled to her feet, extended her hands to the sky, and said the name of her father three times. Only then the pain stopped.

Eurydice ordered us to get up. She motioned us toward the grave. We saw the top of a casket.

Papa Mosso's photo softens in the water and unfurls itself on the ground while Princess is thrown every which way through the *humfo* by the violence of the beatings she has willed upon us.

Clesh opened the casket. With horror we saw a decomposing body dimly lit by the moonlight. Eurydice squatted beside the grave, stroked the repulsive face of the corpse. The stench was nauseating. Eurydice spoke to the dead man. She told us to come forward, to touch him while she went on speaking to him in Creole.

Princess drags herself toward the clay bowls, horrified to see Papa Mosso's photo disintegrating. She pants; her body bleeds, beaten by the billy-club onslaught she had willed upon us and that came back to pummel her after having been deflected by Eurydice's pure body. Princess grabs the dagger, stabs our images with it. The water turns to blood.

We fell in agony. Eurydice screamed three times. She wrapped a black stone in Princess's red tunic and tossed it on the corpse, which seemed to engulf it.

Invisible daggers pierce Princess's body, her blood splashes, the water in the bowls again becomes purified, our images disappear from the surface of the water, and just as the stone falls into the putrefying flesh of the corpse, Princess curls up and dies.

Our pain stopped immediately. Eurydice left us and leaned over Clesh, who was agonizing, stabbed all over. She lay down upon his body, muttering a prayer, but it was too late.

Brad turned off the VCR. Mona and I had tears in our eyes. Brad was ashen. Joe was trembling so bad he spilled his coffee. Nobody said anything. I got up, took Mona by the hand; we walked out of Miami police headquarters. When they saw our faces, Live Crew discreetly put a move on. Eurydice had declined to watch the tape.

      We climbed into the BMW, and I sped out of town, toward the Keys. Three hours later we were crossing the Infinity Bridge, surrounded by an aquamarine sea. I was steering with one hand and with the other stroking Mona, Pussy Queen, future superstar of rap, pressed against me, her beautiful dark eyes lost in the sky.